Necronomicon Cookbook

By Sean-Michael Argo

Copyright 2014 by Sean-Michael Argo
All Rights Reserved

Editing, cover art
and interior design
By TL Bland
Thruterryseyes.com

"Let's dig a hole in the sand brother, a little grave we can fill together."
- The Dead Weathers

Cthulhu F'tagn!

So Mote It Be Ya'll.

WELCOME TO THE BACKWOODS

My name is Clifford Bartlett, a bootlegger and slayer of nasty things. Yessir, I make my living selling moonshine. Well, when I ain't repairing lawnmowers and the like down at my shop, but times are slow so I can't say it's a stable living. I do admit that when I gut me a few cultists I do take a peek at their wallets, though honestly, most of what I make goes into fuel, shotgun shells, and hospital bills.

What you got in your paws right now, is what me and the boys have taken to calling the 'Necronomicon Cookbook', and the way I figure, it's best described as one part Grimoire and one part cookbook. In these pages you'll read about how we cast spells using moonshine, fight monsters with magic shotguns, and then preserve our souls and sanity with some down home cooking.

I thought long and hard about listing all the various shoggoths, dead names, Elder Gods, and various beasties that a body might encounter and ultimately decided to leave them out. Trying to come up with a comprehensive compendium of such things is a fool's errand. There are way too many horrors to compile, and folks who try, go insane in the doing of it. A powerful wizard, Abdul Al Hazrad, known by most as The Mad Arab, made the attempt, and though he gained great power and had himself one hell of an adventure, he bought the farm as messy as it gets.

The storyteller, H.P. Lovecraft, tried to shield his mind by writing it all as fiction, and though it worked for a while, it got him, too. There are others to have done the research and created a product, more than I'll bother to name here, ranging from yuppie New Yorkers, British occultist, to brilliant painters and even musicians. I know that one of these days I'll lose my sanity too, but I figure I'll honor the deeds of those who came before me by letting their work stand.

Think of this book as a supplement to the dusty tomes of folks way smarter than yours truly. Let those books give you the details on who you're fighting, and let this little book of mine help you drink up, pull the trigger, and enjoy a fine meal afterwards.

KNOW THE STAKES

Something you have to know, that you have to get right with before you can walk down this hard road, is that you'll either die messy or eventually go insane.

If you survive long enough, madness is guaranteed. There's no way around it, and trust me lots of folks have tried. Human beings can't be exposed to the mythos without going insane. It's a bit like gravity that way. No matter what you do, it's coming. The best we can hope for is to stave off that crazy for as long as we can, any way that we can, so we can stay in the fight. Therapy doesn't work, because you'll only end up getting committed. Drugs only distract you or numb you into a trance. And who the hell has time for hobbies?

We're in the dirty South, so we do it our way, which is drinking and eating like there's no tomorrow.

Because there most likely ain't.

THE MYTHOS

Darkness Between the Stars, they are asleep in the deep or hiding in the skies, and there's always some yahoo trying to bring 'em here. That's where me, and folks like me, come in. We track down these sorry sons of bitches and put a stop to 'em before the Elder Gods awaken. Needless to say, most law enforcement agencies consider us 'most wanted', but we do what we gotta do.

We call ourselves slayers, or at least that's how me and the boys think of it. There aren't that many of us in the grand scheme of things, but it always seems like there's just enough of us to buy the world a few extra days of life every time some cult gets close to bringing down the curtain. I won't list all of their unholy names here. If you're reading this book you know enough to know it's best not to write such things down.

There are a few copies of the old Necronomicon floating around slayer circles, so those who need to know also know who to call. I used to be a book warden, but after a few years it was hard to even sleep in the same house with the damn thing, and some other poor slayer became its keeper.

Cults are the biggest problem, and the most common. The whispers of the darkness are contagious, and it seems like every time I turn around there's another gang of miscreants sacrificing teenagers and summoning up horrific things. All I can say to that is, God bless Mossberg, Remington, and Colt.

THE DIRTY SOUTH

For whatever reason, almost the whole heap of 'mythos activity' happens in the South. Sure, there's been some things go down out on Rhode Island, a few incursions in Boston, and everybody knows what happened out at Insmouth, but for the most part it's all South of the good ole Mason Dixon Line (which had more witchcraft behind its creation than politics).

You know that whole 'the South will rise again' thing? Yeah, there's a goddamn reason. Hell, we started the damn Civil War to stop the rise of The King in Yellow in Washington, D.C., but politics and the war shifted way out of our favor, and well, you know how it went down, we Southern folks got our asses kicked, but not before we put every one of those cultists on the end of a bayonet and sent the King back to hell.

Sometimes the price is heavy. The South is a rough enough place to live without having to worry about a shoggoth rising up outta the swamp or some pack of cultists snatching you for a human sacrifice. So we do our work, which is a damn sight harder these days. Used to be a slayer could gun down the bad guys and roll on his merry way. That was back in the glory days, when about the closest thing to forensics was dusting for fingerprints. With modern law enforcement being so blasted scientific and technologically advanced, we have to be way more careful. Sadly, we've lost plenty of good men and women to the long arm of the law, since to them, we're just a bunch of killers like all the rest.

You ever listen to Southern music much? From old blues songs to the new rock and folk tunes from younger bands? All them songs are drinking, fighting, cussing, killing, living on the road, and running from the law songs. Our fight with the mythos has left a deep current in the collective subconscious of the South and it bubbles up in our music. The darkness is part of us. We've been living and struggling with it so long, I doubt we'd know what to do if we ever did win.

Though we all know we won't.

Even folks who don't know a damn thing about the mythos have the darkness. It's in the air, in the soil, in the water, in our genes. Booze unlocks part of that in all Southern folk who've got at least one or two generations worth of heritage here. Just sit back at a bar one night, and you'll see it. The trick is to harness that darkness, turn it back around at the things that caused it, and fight the good fight.

The South has always been a hard place. It ain't no coincidence that our music is full of darkness. It all starts with the land. A wise man once said that America was a hard place for gods, and that's proven true ever since the first humans put foot to ground here. The swamps are deadly places, where water and rot rule. Our mountains are beaten down to their bare bones, and their secrets lie just beneath the surface, sometimes even in plain sight. You count up the cities in the world known for their 'occult history' and we top that list more than once, and that's just the famous places.

There are the cities you know, hotbeds of Mythos and occult activity, each with their own flavor that's known to folk, all bubbling with tentacle cults, black magic, and worse. Places like New Orleans, Savannah, or Memphis. Then you have the places few folks know about, but are flooded with mojo just the same. Places like Eureka Springs, Arkansas, Lake Charles, Louisiana, or Mobile, Alabama. There's also the mountains, mostly the Ozarks and the Appalachians, with all their hidden cave systems and xenophobic clans of hill folk. Basically, anywhere there's poverty and standing water you'll find Mythos activity, and really, that's a good general rule of thumb.

The swamp states, like Louisiana, Georgia, and Alabama are usually ate up with horrors from the deep. The rest of the South, from the mountains of Virginia to the dusty plains of Oklahoma, are typically under assault from the things that hide in the darkness between the stars and the horrors that walk in the light of the moon. Texas, Arizona, and New Mexico have their own flavor of horror too, because there were dark blood gods in those jungles and mesas for nearly as long as the Deep Ones and the Outer Dark, and they've been at war since the beginning.

The European conquerors might have committed some heinous crimes against humanity, and that's a damn shame, but I reckon that the world is better off with a little bit less human sacrifice. Especially since some of those blood gods got devoured and replaced with agents of the Elder Gods. The last thing anybody needs is an entire civilization worshiping a god who has been secretly supplanted by the Enemy. Obviously there's crossover all the time, but that's kinda the breaks.

The Native Americans who chose to stay in the South were in constant war with each other and the mythos. The forests and swamps were haunted by shoggoth and specters, while in the rivers and lakes swam snakes and gar fish that had no righteous origin. When the white man showed up with his carpenter god and his guns, for awhile it looked like we were gonna take this place for our own, but just like the natives before we got sucked into the spiritual mulch and even as we shaped the place to suit us, it shaped us too.

Multitude of tribes in Africa, where the darkness of the Mythos is known by other hungry names. Immigrant folk, who carried with them the ancient secrets of the Celts and the Gypsies, started mixing it up with slave folk who were slinging voodoo from the Caribbean and Santeria from South America, and all of them on the land of the native Osage, Quapaw, Seminole, and other tribes. The druid met the Houngan and the Brujo met the medicine man, and some of these interactions resulted in violence, others in hybrid cults of one god or another, and precious few yielded the men and women we now know as slayers.

It makes a kind of sense that Hastur and his boy, Narlhythotep, keep coming at us down here, because in the South, we are sitting on top of something, a kinda doorway, and they want to open it. The land rests up on a gateway, part physical and part spiritual, and there's a kind of radiation from it, tainting everything. It's that darkness we talk about, palpable for us all the time, and found in the music, the art, and even our food for those who look hard enough. The gate is here, so the fight is here, and that's why we're here. Its part of our DNA by now, been here enough generations, especially since we've come by it honest thanks to our ancestors who came here from one tribe or another. While racism is still alive and well in the South, you'll never find a drop of it in the loose knit slayer community, for us there's human and there's Mythos, and for us that's what matters.

THE CULTS OF EVIL MEN

There will always be men who aren't content with the world as it is. They've got this itch deep in their soul that don't seem to ease up no matter how much they scratch it. Lord knows I'm one of 'em, but having that itch ain't what's important, its what a man does about it that counts. At least that's what my daddy used to say, and just to make sure I didn't think more of him than was fair, he'd follow it up by saying he planned to light the world on fire when he was a young man, only to find that his book of matches was wet.

If you spend a few hours watching the news, reading the paper, or listening to the talking heads on the radio, you'll get the sense that there's a lot of folks who ain't happy with how things are, but they aren't who I'm talking about. Those folks are chasing illusions and don't even realize it, things like money, fame, bigger homes, better cars, more attractive lovers. It's a constant back and forth as people wrestle to get more than what they have or keep what they already got.

None of that matters to the man with the itch.

This game is about power, and for such men it's the only one worth playing. These men know it's all a sideshow, and some of them learn how to see through it. In doing so, they are exposed to the horrors that comprise true reality. Those horrors fill them with truth and power and purpose. Such men will always gather, they will form covenants with each other and with things much darker than even themselves, and they will conspire. When the illusions of the day to day world suit their needs, they'll support the lies of commerce, government, and law. When those illusions do not suit them, then they'll sow chaos, hedonism, and anarchy.

They are the most fearsome of enemies because we often don't know who they are until folks have already died and their plans are already in motion. More often than not, they are hiding in plain sight, so to engage them means to be at odds with the long arm of the law. The worst of it is that we must take care not to learn too much about them, even as we fight them, because their madness and darkness is a contagious thing. I have no idea what kinds of rituals or schemes are being run by this cult or that, and I don't wanna know. A good slayer will learn how to see the context clues, gain just enough knowledge to see the signs, but taking care not to lean too heavy on that slippery slope. The clues are all around us, if you can train yourself to see them, and for once this actually makes the news a useful thing.

Even an old fart like me knows how to surf the internet, even if I still like my ink and paper news on Sunday mornings. The most obvious clue is a sudden rash of disappearances, even if that's the most depressing part of the process. You see, when cults first start off there are usually only a handful of wicked folk who are huddling up around either a mortal leader or a manifested horror. The kinds of rituals and workings they're most likely to do only need one or two human sacrifices. Heck sometimes they'll just do in a few animals and that'll get 'em what they need. The sad fact is, that when a cult reaches a point where they are doing mass killings, it means that they are near the apex of their power, the big bad mojo rite is nearly complete and basically you are already working against the clock from the moment you discover them.

Sometimes you get lucky and stumble across something before it gets too bad, but trust me, friend, it always starts with a body, and no amount of hope, prayer, or kicking ass is gonna change that. In the face of that bleakness, there are a few hardy folk who have stepped up to become seers, folks like Papa Proctor and The Grin. These guys were sorcerers once, and still are when they're backs are against the wall, but for one reason or another they've turned their eyes to the stars and the darkness in between. In those crooked spaces, where the light doesn't always shine, they can see things that you and I can't ever see, and wouldn't want to anyway. To hear them describe the experience it's like seeing an infinity of possible outcomes while being swaddled in the embrace of the earth and then getting hit in the face with a lightning bolt.

Needless to say, I won't be asking again, I just take their word for it. Can't always trust what they're gonna tell you. They'd be the first ones to point that out, because they aren't just prophets standing on the sidelines, nope they're in the shit just as deep as we are, even if not a bit deeper, so nothing you get from them is going to be objective. Every now and then these guys get lucky and catch something on the ether before too many victims pile up, and they'll reach out, sometimes to the first slayer they can find, or they'll move mountains to connect with the slayer that it seems fate has deemed to be 'the guy'. Personally, I think its bullshit at least half the time, but I've seen enough to know that I don't know a damn thing for sure, and so when I get the call, I take it. The hope is always that you can catch up to the cult before they've got too much power, so that you're fighting just men.

If they've accumulated enough mojo they could have summoned shoggoth allies, thrown hexes that are stronger than moonshine, and even have drawn in some of the bigger players like Narlythotep or his boss Hastur.

As I've said, I ain't naming names except for these two bastards. There are a few cults here and there, usually small, I've noticed, who worship gods with names that have way too many consonants. The occasional small coastal town will have a religious hard-on for this fish-god or that squid-god, but the big cults are always Hastur's boys. The Cult of the Yellow Sign. I swear, it's like these guys are the mega-churches of the Mythos.

Legends tell that Narlythotep roams the South as a vagabond musician, playing his spooky tunes in whatever dive bar or juke joint he happens to be near when the sun starts to set. He's always on the bill, and nobody ever seems to think that's weird, until its too late. According to the stories, ole Narlythotep starts all the Yellow Sign cults by choosing someone to be the high priest, teaching them the secrets, granting them power, then moving on down the road.

I've even heard stories that the ultimate goal is, if enough cults complete a grand rite called 'The Repairing of Reputations' in a particular pattern, across the land, at that point Hastur will come end the world. Its always something like that, a cult rises, victims bleed, and the dark gods rise. Obviously, they ain't succeeded yet because we're all still here, but they've come close a few times and I'd wager that we're never more than one or two grand rites away from the end.

I'd know more and be able to tell you more, except knowledge like that corrupts the mind, soul, and even the body, so you, me, and every other seer and slayer has to work on half-truths, rumors, and outright tall tales. At the end of the day, just squeeze the trigger and don't worry so much about the details, because you're better off just dousing it in gasoline and sitting down to a chicken dinner while it all burns.

GETTING RIGHT WITH THE MAN UPSTAIRS

Whomever you choose to believe in, worship, or just say hello to every now and then will be a damn sight better than the alternative.

Here's the difference between a slayer and the average man striding this pitiful planet: We know that there's gods out there, lots of em, and they're all real.

I used to hear a saying back in Sunday school, and in my years I've seen the truth of it, that there ain't no atheists alive who've met the devil face to face.

Brother, that shit will make you a believer faster than any burning bush. It's a sad fact that most of us, slayers and good folk alike, are more likely to believe in the bad, to accept it as real, than we are the good. It's part of that flaw they call 'human nature', and its been the cause of more than one conflagration of suck, the worst of which is the bleak cynicism of the modern man.

BRING AN APPETITE

You gotta eat your weight in calories to keep this up. Not only is it a physically hard job, but casting spells and dealing with the crazy that

the mythos will put on you, that takes vitality out of ya. That's why Southern Cooking is so full of fat and fried goodness.
Did you think we called it 'soul food' for no reason?

Over the generations we've lost the truth behind that kind of food, and fewer and fewer good folk are fighting that fight, but for those of us who remember, eating a plate of fried chicken and washing it down with moonshine and lemonade is a sacred thing. Keeps your body going, keeps your mind right, and tastes like a slice of fried heaven. We slayers call it 'cleansing', and it's the most important thing you'll ever learn about fighting the creatures and cultists of the Mythos.

Food, when prepared with intent and focused energy, with the right ingredients and tastes that correspond, is transformed into a soul salve that washes away the darkness.

DIY TILL YOU DIE

Doing your own hunting, fishing, and farming is the best way to get the most mojo. Self-brew, self-grow, catch or kill game, and you're on the hoodoo highway my friend. Sadly though, for a lot of us slayers, there ain't always time or opportunity to produce our own food. Sure, there are a handful of farms and deer camps, run by good people, that cater to slayers. Now, I'm no fool, and I'm not gonna mention any of 'em here. Even if you're one of the good guys reading this book, you're gonna get killed one of these days, and this book could just as easily fall into the wrong hands. I don't mind telling it like it is, but I can't have any of these sanctuaries getting the fire called down on 'em because I did some name dropping.

That being said, these sanctuaries are few and far between, but if you can get tight with someone who knows someone, then these are mighty fine places. Most of em are just farmhouses out in the country where one or two folks live full time, growing gardens or tending livestock, and usually nearby to woods for game or a body of water for fishing. Good places to hole up after a fight, when you're on the run, or need a pretty lady to serve you up a home cooked meal. If you aren't near one of these place, or don't know of one, then buying factory farmed food at the grocery store is about your only option. That kind of food will fill you up, keep your body running, and give you a little mojo, but the whole factory farming process robs food of its magic.

Now I'll admit that I'm a little more paranoid than even your average conspiracy guy, but knowing what I know about pigs and lite beer, I'd have to say that factory farming has got to have a tentacle wrapped around it somewhere in the process. Industry and commerce are powerful forces, and its likely that the whole thing got started by regular men looking to increase their profits, but somewhere along the way the agents of darkness got into the mix. It's like a Farmageddon out there.

When animal's don't get a chance to live even a half-assed animal life, then there ain't much magic in 'em by the time they get to your table. In the 80's and 90's it got real bad, for nearly twenty years if you weren't finding your food at the country store, when you could find one that had managed to stay in business despite the constant price war with Wal-Mart, then you were eating fast food to get your cleanse on the go and sucking down Night Train for your hexing. Hard times those, but things have gotten a hell of a lot better now. God Bless the Yuppies and the Hipsters, who used the power of consumer demand to create organic food sections in major grocery stores, farmer's markets in parking lots, and making it legal to buy beer on Sundays. I tell ya, those skinny jeans wearing, iPhone carrying, granola munching, sardonic-ironic sumbitches are pulling us back from the brink.

So, next time you see some thirty-something manboy and his fedora wearing girlfriend parking a scooter outside your favorite dive bar, buy him a round and make him feel like a regular, even if you can't understand why in the hell he's wearing a scarf in the summertime.

Dumbass.

HEXIN'

We put the shine in moonshine.

Ever wondered where that word 'moonshine' come from?

The Thing that lives in the Moon-light casts its gaze upon the world through that silvery light and trust me, on those nights it's best to stay inside. At some point in the way back, some sorcerers, crazy motherfuckers the lot of 'em, figured out that they could steal that magick and use it to fight the Mythos.

There's the slow and deep magick of Life and Earth, and then there's the Shine. Moonshine is all about breaking rules, shattering conventions, and bending reality around yourself. The magick of the earth is slow and deep, and for lots of slayers that kind of patience and surrender is tough to manage, and so we drink the god's white lightning and do it our way.

When you pull energy from the world and use your will to craft it into useful patterns, that's called magick. We say magick with a 'k' so that folks know we mean mojo, juju, witchcraft, sorcery, and so on. Not the sleight of hand and coin tricks you'll see on street corners and Vegas stages. What follows is the most concise explanation of magick what's ever been put together in one place.

 Now, I've never met the author of these passages, his name was Seth Cardorra, and this is from his book "Chaos Magick". There were whispers about him being one of the more epic badasses of his day, back in the 60's, running around smacking down shoggoths and high priests while giving the phrase 'flower power' a new kind of meaning (his drink of choice was elder-flower wine).

Like other sorcerers, the man was just a little bit too powerful for his own good and ended up becoming a corrupt monster that had to be put down. Tyrone Mitchell, a slayer legend in his own right, caught up with Seth at a condemned hotel in downtown Atlanta on August 14th, 1979.

Seth Cardorra had been smuggling these things called 'plague arks' into the city for weeks, causing outbreaks of nightmare induced insanity that drove those affected into murderous frenzies. When confronted by Mitchell, he screeched that his arks revealed creatures and agents of the Mythos, and that he was forcing open the eyes of the masses, which may have been true. Several shoggoth rampages were triggered (and subsequently put down by either Seth or Tyrone) by these nightmare crazies rooting out the monsters and dying messily once they found them. Lots of the nightmare crazies ended up attacking folks who later turned out to have been cult members of the Yellow Sign.

It's easy to see how Seth thought he was fighting the good fight, but he was doing it with the blood and bodies of normal people, ignorant of the truth and never given the chance to choose. Slayers have a choice, after a fashion, and there's nothing like sacrificing the very people we're trying to save to put you on our black list.

Tyrone had two brothers who went into that hotel with him to face the sorcerer, and after it was all said and done, only Tyrone came out. He died in the driveway of his home, when all of his major organs finally gave up after whatever heinous hexin' Seth had laid on him. The tough bastard lived long enough to say goodbye to his wife before falling to the ground. That was in my younger days and I was guarding Tyrone's family, as Seth had figured out who was hunting him.

I went back to the hotel and the place was crawling with cops, but after they left the scene, around eight hours later, I snuck in. They'd moved the bodies, but hadn't had time to move away all of the spent brass, lakes of carnage, and the shit-smeared symbols all over the walls.

The point of the story is, that you can be a good man, you can fight the good fight, but still turn sour if you go too far, too fast. Still, a man's final deeds don't wash away his earlier ones, and Seth wrote a hell of a book on magick and the occult. This here is a passage from his text, explaining the basic principles of magick.

1. All energy is potential magickal energy.
2. Magick is the use of will to elicit change in energy towards a desired end.
3. The ability to use magick is directly affected by belief.
4. The power of magick depends upon the focus of the user.

"All energy is potential magickal energy."

This is the principle that shows the homogeneity of magickal energy in all magickal traditions of the world. Most cultures have a word that is a close approximation of magickal energy. Some cultures call this energy "mana" others call it "chi", and some just call it "juice". There are many names for the magickal energy that these cultures believe permeates the world. They also believe it's there to be accessed by those who have the ability to do so.

The fact that every magick-using culture has some idea of a magickal energy shows a commonality. Physics shows that all natural events involve a transformation of energy from one form to another, but the amount of energy does not change in the transformation. The law of conservation of energy shows us that matter and energy can neither be created nor destroyed. Albert Einstein showed that all matter is energy. If everything in creation is energy in some form, including magickal energy, and energy cannot be created or destroyed, only transformed, then it can be said that all energy is potential magickal energy.

"Magick is the use of will to elicit change in energy towards a desired end."

This is the principle that deals with the actual act of magick. Of the four principles, this is the one that is found in every culture almost with-out exception. Many cultures see some-one using magick as an individual acting apart from society or religion in order to achieve some personal goal. When acting alone, the only tool one has is their will. The process of magick, the act of using one's will to do magick, is morally neutral. The moral implications of magick fall upon the shoulders of the magick-user, not the magick itself. Through the use of will, changes are made in energy that, provided the will is strong enough, result in the desired outcome. Much like it takes will to sit in Buddhist meditation for hours on end, it takes will to summon up magickal energy and use it to cause changes in reality.

"The ability to use magick is directly affected by belief."

This principle of magick is the principle what illustrates the dynamic nature of magick. It can be inferred from this principle that if a person does not believe that they are capable of magick then they won't be able to do it.

One might argue that experiences like the Kundalini awakening, a phenomenon entailing the abundant rising of potent spiritual energy from the base of the spine, happens regardless of belief in magick. While Kundalini is a magickal experience, the person experiencing the awakening is not, at that moment, willworking. The awakening does, however, greatly encourage the belief in such things as more energy openings occur in the person. These eventually develop into the Kundalini powers, including psycho kinesis and telepathy, which are, at their most basic, non-cultural nature, magick.

The ability to use magick is not only about capability, but style. The way in which one believes magick works greatly shapes one's ability to use it. For instance, many Satanists believe that their powers come from studying texts and initiation rituals. Many of them even believe that their leaders and demonic allies grant powers to them. They also believe that such powers can be taken away from them. Many practitioners of Vodoun also believe that their powers are granted to them in some form by the Loa. There are other magick-users who belong to a group known as the Hermetic Order of the Golden Dawn, who believe that magickal ability is a measure of one's will, and that the only limiting factor is the strength of that will. If one strips culture away from this principle, it can be seen that belief shapes the ability to use magick, which is a commonality among most cultures.

"The power of magick depends upon the focus of the user."

This principle is perhaps the most broad of the four principles. This principle deals with several elements of focus. One of the elements of focus is the ability of the magick-user to gather various amounts magickal energy and shape it into the desired form without losing control of the summoned energy.

An example of this would be, a Teutonic sorcerer attempting to write rune script upon the blade of a sword. The more magickal energy the sorcerer puts into the drawing of the runes, the more powerful they will become. If the sorcerer tries to use more energy than he or she can control and still cast the spell, then something undesirable might happen, such as the sword breaking or the spell simply not working. Many people believe that this is one of the many roles played by rituals. Aside from their social functions, rituals provide the magick-user with a specific way to go about using magick.

Many psychologist and sociologist have showed that human beings like order. To be more specific, human beings like maps. The rituals serve as maps for the magick-users to keep in mind while they work their magick; it is a tool for deepening one's concentration and energy controlling capa-city. Because of this, magickal tradition says that ritual is a tool to be used until the magick-user is capable of causing the same changes without the use of ritual, that they are metaphor-ical training wheels in a way. For these traditions, the more internalized rituals become, the less one has need for them.

The other element of focus is the perceived source of the magickal energy being utilized by the magick-user. Many magick-users focus on drawing the magickal energy from within their own being, in essence they see themselves as their own power source. Others focus on drawing their energy from specific deities. This is not to say that the above sort of focus applies to those people who coerce spirits for aid. This focus applies to the practitioners of theurgy. For theurgist, the magickal energy that they use comes directly through the deity that they are focusing upon. An example of this would be a Catholic priest performing an exorcism upon a possessed person; by invoking the power of God the priest is able to shape that power and use his will to cast the demon out.

POWER IN THE SPIRITS

Elements of Earth

Gin - Health and Vitality spells - also useful as a combination ingredient for other elixirs oriented towards the maintenance, healing, and armoring of the body. Can also be spit or finger drawn onto associated symbolic or practical items such as body armor, first aid materials, or seatbelts. Been shot, cut, bruised, stabbed, or other-wise mauled? Want to protect yourself from it in the first place? Pour some gin on the rocks or mix up a refreshing cocktail.

Beer, Wine, and Mead - Family and Community are The areas of spell work that these spirits lend Themselves towards. Each is made with time, care, and attention, all carrying the flavor and mojo of the land and the people that crafted them. Hence, again, the push towards only using micro-brew beer, mead, and the more intimately created wines. It's easy to buy the cheap stuff, but you get what you pay for my friend. This is the 'from my table to yours' kind of boozing and should be approached in this way as much as possible. I know it might feel like you're being a hipster about it, but they're onto something, and that something has power.

Element of Water

Rum - Gaining Favor or Commerce orient-ed spells, especially when one is attempting to engage in bribery, coercion, or barter. Useful in creating offerings to spirits of idea, element, or place. Need to pull some 'smooth operator' moves with the locals? Think you might need to bribe your way out of a prison cell, or call on the aid of a friendly spirit? Grab a bottle of rum and be generous with the portions, for yourself and your 'friends'.

Element of Earth and Water

Vodka - Relentlessness and Cold Courage are the flavors of this spirit, and the spells cast with it reflect its in-tractable nature. When you need to imbue yourself with the power to carry on no matter what the odds, no matter the pain, no matter the cost. When you must be brave, but near callous in your courageous-ness. Do you need to be The Terminator? Are you going to have to fight through a wall of pain and suffering only to find more of the same on the other side? Here's a vodka martini. I mixed it dirty, just like you.

Element of Air

Absinthe - Divination spells, out of body astral travel. Consume prior to workings, or incorporate anointing or dipping the finger to draw symbols. You wanna read your future or take a spiritual walkabout? Get a few sugar cubes and drink up.

Element of Fire

Tequila - Mastery of the Present Moment kind of spells, the sort of spells that give you an edge when you need to be at the apex of the perfect union of luck, timing, and daring. Do you need to have your own heist movie? Comprised of a complex series of perfectly executed bold moves that all come together in a web of amazing success, all done with a non-existent margin of error? Do you need to 'do it now' and make it 'epic'? Then have yourself a few tequila shooters, a tequila sunrise, or maybe a margarita on the rocks and make some amazing shit happen, Right Now. Remember, though, that hangovers are a bitch, and in this game coming up snake eyes means you die bloody. This is the all-or-nothing-right-fucking-now spirit.

Element of Fire and Air

Whiskey - Defiance and Paradox. This spirit is the power behind spells that push you towards heights not typically possible even as the spirit itself drags you down. You are made stronger and weaker, sharper in some ways and yet blunted in other ways. This liquor is all about changing the way things are, but at a cost, and it's always temporary. Are you keenly aware of the fact that you are facing down the most ancient of evils and you are but a simple man of no special significance? It doesn't matter once you pound half a pint of whiskey. You'll fight and die like an 80's action hero. Up is down and down is up, above is below and below is above, but only so long as you walk the line. When you sober up it's all going to just be a jumble of broken glass and spent brass, but goddamn, when you're in the hurricane of a whiskey drunk it is sublime.

ALCHEMICAL MIXOLOGY

This is just a quick list of the better known and most effective cocktails. The more attention and intent you put into mixing your cocktail the more powerful its effects will be. This is a big reason that most slayers like a good craft beer, and those who can, will homebrew a batch whenever they have the time and resources. Prepare the beverage with your intended effects in mind, then enjoy drinking it as you visualize the spirit infusing you with the spells you've concocted. As soon as that first edge of the buzz hits your system you know it's time to rock and roll.

Mint Julep

2 cups water
2 cups white sugar
1/2 cup roughly chopped fresh mint leaves
32 ozs. Kentucky bourbon
8 sprigs fresh mint leaves for garnish

Combine water, sugar and chopped mint leaves in a small saucepan. Bring to a boil over high heat until the sugar is completely dissolved. Allow syrup to cool, approximately 1 hour. Pour syrup through a strainer to remove mint leaves. Fill eight cups or frozen goblets with crushed ice and pour 4 ounces of bourbon and 1/4 cup mint syrup in each. (Proportions can be adjusted depending on each person's sweet tooth). Top each cup with a mint sprig and a straw.

Sloe Gin Fizz

2 ice cubes
2 ozs. sloe gin
1 oz lemon juice
1 tsp simple syrup
1 cup ice
4 ozs. club soda
1 slice lemon

Place 2 ice cubes in a highball glass. Set aside in the freezer. Combine sloe gin, lemon juice, and simple syrup in a cocktail shaker. Add ice, cover and shake until chilled. Strain into the prepared highball glass. Stir in club soda. Garnish with a slice of lemon.

Tom Collins

1 1/2 cups ice
2 ozs. gin
3/4 oz lemon juice
1/2 oz simple syrup
1 cup ice
2 ozs. club soda
1 lemon wedge

Fill a Collins glass with 1 1/2 cups ice, set aside in the freezer. Combine gin, lemon juice, and simple syrup in a cocktail shaker. Add 1 cup ice, cover and shake until chilled. Strain into the chilled Collins glass. Top with club soda and garnish with a lemon wedge.

Sidecar

Ice cubes
1/2 oz freshly squeezed
lemon juice
1 oz brandy
1/2 oz Cointreau or Triple Sec
1 lemon wedge

Fill a cocktail shaker 3/4 full with ice cubes. Pour in lemon juice, Contreau and brandy. Cover and shake vigorously for about 30 seconds until the outside of the shaker becomes cold and frosty. Strain into a martini glass and garnish with a wedge of lemon.

Hot Toddy

1 tsp honey
2 ozs. boiling water
1 1/2 ozs. whiskey
3 whole cloves
1 cinnamon stick
1 slice lemon
1 pinch ground nutmeg

Pour the honey, boiling water, and whiskey into a mug. Spice it with the cloves and cinnamon, and put in the slice of lemon. Let the mixture stand for 5 minutes so the flavors can mingle, then sprinkle with a pinch of nutmeg before serving.

Manhattan

2 ozs. bourbon
1/2 oz sweet vermouth

1 maraschino cherry (optional)
1/2 cup ice

Place ice into a shaker, and pour the vermouth and bourbon over the ice. Mix well. Pour drink into a cocktail glass, and garnish with a cherry.

WRONG TURNS COST

When me and Ronnie Fix rolled up on a trailer house that was down about forty miles of Louisiana dirt roads and switchbacks, we knew it was the place. I had my usual load out, plus a bullet-proof vest I scored from my buddy Jeff, a retired deputy from south Arkansas.

Ronnie never much liked vests, crazy sumbitch, but he made up for it with the kind of wicked fast draw you don't expect from a bigger guy. We knew this had to be the place, and not just from the weird ass scarecrows and bloody symbols drawn across the walls, but from the overwhelming sense of evil we could feel vibrating around the place. Ronnie's no hexer, but even he could feel it.

Usually, we open up with a one liner or some other kinda bravado, but it just didn't seem right in this place. Bad things had happened to good people here, and the trouble weren't near done. We had been rolling with the headlights off for the last mile or two, letting the light of the full moon do its thing.

We'd shut off the truck a few hundred yards back and hiked in on foot, and I'm glad we made that call. The cult had set spikes all across the road at about fifty yards in, just outside the tree line. We decided to move around to the back of the property, inside the tree line. Ya never knew when one of those corrupted bastards might be looking down rifle sights. As we came around we could see the nightmare we'd come here to stop.

Behind the trailer there was a row of dog cages, maybe a dozen of them, set up in a circle around a handmade wooden table. The table was covered in old gore and buzzing with flies. Leaning against it was the biggest sledge-hammer I'd ever seen.

I whispered something along the lines of backstage passes to a sick ass Gallagher show and Ronnie shot me a dirty look. Guess he didn't appreciate the humor. We could see that about half the cages had naked people in them. None of them were moving, whether they were asleep or unconscious we couldn't tell, but they were all in various stages of hurt and neglect.

Now here was the dirty shame of it, every one of those folks had friends and kin, but it wasn't until some local politician's daughter got taken that it hit the news. We try to keep tabs on what happens beneath the notice of mainstream media, but there's only so many plates we can catch before one hits the floor. Ronnie caught wind of it in the paper, then from there we were able to link the disappearances with the moon phases and pick up on a Hastur pattern.

Kinda helped that a Yellow Sign token had been left in the girl's apartment. Cults usually have to leave tokens in

the home of their victims, an energetic exchange of sorts, like they are taking that person and their 'hearth'. Holistic human sacrifice. Yup, I wouldn't have believed it either had I not seen the things I have.
Hastur.

It seems like it's always that moonlit bastard. Makes sense though, as he and his boy, Narlythotep, are the harbingers of the Old Ones, so I guess I shouldn't get pissy about it and just cowboy up.

Ronnie and I did our best to move silently through the camp, not wanting to be noticed by the folks in the cages any more than the whackos in the trailer. We're some tough customers sure, but there was only two of us, so we weren't taking any chances. He took the right and I took the left, and we moved on the trailer. Now if we were cops, we mighta knocked first, or maybe told 'em to come out with their hands up, but that ain't us.

I cocked my 'masterkey shotgun' and used it on the doorknob.

As the door blew back I stepped inside and spoke the words. I'd had myself two strong as a mule boiler-makers before we let the car, and I was feeling good. The power leapt out of me, and as the hex filled the trailer I was able to see which of the occupants were corrupted and which were normal folk.

Normally, Ronnie and I would have just set the trailer on fire and shot everyone who ran out, but we knew there was a damn good chance there would be civilians in there, more kidnap victims being used for all manner of messed up things. Our hunch was spot on, as I saw six of the black-eyed bastards looking at me, and two uncorrupted folks, a man and a woman, tied to a chair.

The cultists had those black eyes that all of them do when you're looking at them through the hex, and their skin was all cracked and dry, with what looked like a black mold in all the folds and creases in their skin.

Disgusting right?

For a second we just stood there, them staring at me and me at them. For them it was probably the surprise of knowing someone could see them for what they were, for me it was the usual shock of encroaching madness that al-ways comes with seeing this kind of horror. Thankfully, my blood alcohol level was high enough that it only stopped me for a second, and I yelled out, "Two in the chair!" before cutting loose with the masterkey once again.

I blasted the top half of one guy clean off. Musta hit the guy next to him with a few pellets of shot because he went down too, screaming. I managed to duck back out the door as the others got their wits about them and started shooting back.

I gotta admit, I'm getting a little old and those were some damn strong cocktails, so I missed my footing duck-ing out and pretty much fell off the stairs onto the dirt.
Not the slayer I used to be, but I still have a few tricks, and was able to get my belly gun in hand as I

rolled onto my back. I got lucky 'cause the first one didn't notice where I'd fallen right off. By the time he did, I'd put two rounds in his chest. His buddy, clever sumbitch, used the corpse as a human shield and shot met in the thigh.

Better lucky than good is what they say, because the round was small caliber and didn't shred me up. I pushed him back into the trailer by emptying my gun into him and his shield, then let out a, "Hell, yeah!" when a round from inside the trailer punched a hole through his skull.

Ronnie stepped out, gun smoking, and a grim look on his face and told me the victims didn't make it out of the crossfire. I said that was how it went sometimes, much as it pissed me off that we'd tried so hard.

Didn't help that I'm the only guy on God's earth who can wear a bullet proof vest and manage to get shot in the thigh.

We set fire to the trailer and got the folks out of the cages. I doubt they'll ever recover, even though we got 'em a good supper laid out. Most of 'em will likely commit suicide or get committed, poor folks. Who knows though, sometimes surviving a thing like that is exactly how a person decides to become a slayer. Once you see the tentacles behind the curtain, your choices are breaking or fighting back.

Madness is guaranteed.

WAR STORIES

There's a phrase I've heard thrown around and over the years. I've heard it said a dozen different ways, but it goes something along the lines of "The only way to tell if a war story is true, is how it makes you feel". It strikes me as a twenty dollar way of saying that the truth is relative, and to communicate the essence of a thing, sometimes you gotta jazz it up a bit. For example, I'll tell you about the rise and fall of Nathaniel, aka 'Papa Proctor', and you're likely to miss the point entirely, because I'm gonna tell you how it all really happened.

The factual account of Papa Proctor goes like this: On August 6th, 1945, at 8:16 a.m., while the B-29 bomber Enola Gay was dropping the world's first nuclear bomb on the Japanese city of Hiroshima, a young Arkansas woman named Elizabeth Lynne Proctor gave birth to a baby boy.

Upon setting eyes on him, she screamed and died of a heart attack and severe brain hemorrhaging, leaving Nathaniel Alan Proctor an orphan. His father, an unknown blues musician and drifter who had long since disappeared.

Nate grew up in a small orphanage in Des Arc, Arkansas, that was more of a work camp than a place to raise children. He had an obsession with blues music and the men who played it, often sneaking out of the orphanage to hear the bluesmen play in the seedy clubs that dotted the White River just at the edge of town.

By the time Nate was seventeen, he was an emancipated youth who worked at being a farmhand and doing odd jobs while living in the rental group flophouse maintained by the same folks who ran the orphanage. He was a frequent guest at the city jail, and known to be a boozer and a brawler, even at such a tender age. Being a strange boy, who seemed to have a special connection with animals, among other small manifestations of power, he was a defiant loner with no friends or family to speak of.

On his eighteenth birthday Nate was one of the only survivors of a tragic fire at one of the seedy music joints. For those who gained Nate's confidence years later, he explained that it was a harrowing attack caused by a wandering blues musician who served Hastur.
That night was the pivotal moment in Nate's life. From then on he followed the long hard road of a slayer. He moved to Northwest Arkansas and eventually met Molly Jansen, fathered two daughters and adopted a third.

When the girls were still in diapers, Molly was attacked by someone who packed her mouth with salt, blindfolded her with a leather belt, poured gasoline all over her, and lit her on fire. Nate was initially charged with her murder, put on trial, and found guilty by Judge Isaac C. Parker, who, despite being from Fort Smith and out of his jurisdiction in Fayetteville, sat in judgment of Nate's case. Judge Parker was known as 'The Hanging Judge', but in a rare decision, decided to sentence Nate as 'time served' and sent him on his way.

Nate soon made an alliance with the bush wizard known as 'The Grin', who taught Nate about the art of hexing and the deeper mysteries of the Mythos. By the time he met me, Clifford Bartlett, and we partnered up to wipe out a Cthulhu cult that had taken control of the high society of Eureka Springs, who were already a bizarre bunch to begin with, Nate had read the Gospel of the Tentacle and taken to calling himself 'Papa' Proctor.

After a number of years and several more violent encounters with the Mythos, many involving his own daughters, whom he trained up to be slayers them-selves, Nate, then known by all but myself as Papa Proctor, went insane. He killed Jefferson Teague, a well-known slayer from Kentucky, in a hexin' duel over a cause as yet unknown to anyone but Proctor and Teague, and disappeared into the forests of the Ozarks. Local slayer lore holds that 'the owls are not what they seem' and that Papa Proctor still resides somewhere in the forests, moving his campsite every dawn, and watching the world through the eyes of his owl familiars after dark.

Now, if I'd wanted to tell you the truth, to make you understand who Papa Proctor really is and why if you ever meet him you're destined for terror and glory, I would've had to change a few things, swap some facts with fiction, modify some of the details, to tell it the way it needs to be told. Most of our stories are like obituaries mixed with a few urban legends and wrapped in a Greek tragedy, and that's how you gotta tell 'em to communicate the truth. As it is, probably best you just stick to the facts when it comes to Papa Proctor, decent people, even those of us who call ourselves slayers, shouldn't think too much on such things.

Sometimes the truth is best left to lie.

THE MASTERKEY

For every slayer you talk to, there will be a different opinion about what sort of firearms are the best for our kind of work. As far as I'm concerned, anything that'll put a man in the ground is good enough for me, but if I have my preference, I'm a shotgun man all the way. Most of us old timers use the shotgun, as it's easier and cheaper to mix the mojo into your bullets, though some of the more resourceful young bucks have found ways to infuse their bullets. Takes all kinds, but I like to stick with what I know, and dammit I'm the one writing this book, so we're gonna talk shotguns.

I like to call mine the 'Masterkey', since there's rarely a door that I can't open with it. Blast off the lock, shoot out the hinges, or I could just knock a hole through the middle. I do admit that over the years I have swapped out my heavy hunting shotgun for a lighter weight tactical shotgun, with a folding stock and a trigger handle, easier on these old shoulders of mine.

Most of the time I stick to buckshot, since more often than not, I'm outnumbered and fighting in tight spaces, and that's when buckshot works its magic. You pump a few loads of shot into a room packed with furniture and cultists and you'll have whipped your-self up a fine soup made out of splinters and body parts. Hell of a mess to clean up though, but that's why I al-ways have a can of gas in the back of my truck.

There's a conjure man who used to live out in the swamps near the town of DeValls Bluff, that made the best shot-gun rounds in the south. Everybody would swear by him, and those lucky few of us who have some boxes of his shells still swear by him. Never knew what his real name was, always just called him Conjure Man, and he liked it that way. He ended up on the wrong end of a poison fugu needle back when the loup garou were rampaging out there, before the Bartlett Boys and Danny Jenkins handled business.

Conjure was a good man, but if I've learned anything in my years, it's that good men die hard. No passing peace-fully in our sleep, and I reckon that's alright with me. Already having trouble moving in the mornings, and cold weather makes my joints so stiff I have to get my shine on just to move around okay.

Honestly, it's a miracle I haven't gotten liver cancer yet. Maybe it's all the mojo in the booze that keeps things working, who knows. Anyway, me and Conjure once holed up in his swamp shack for a week working on making ammo. He would use an engraver to etch veve (that's a fancy word for magical symbols, bringing down the fire and general badassery of the voodoo spirits) onto the shells while I re-armed them with a salt, iron shavings, and steel shot mix. We use the salt and iron because you never know when the creep you're blasting is more shoggoth than human.

Salt has natural properties that dispel and disperse magical energy, which not only makes is very important when it comes to cooking cleansing food, but also for dropping bad guys. The salt hits 'em and makes it harder for the dark creatures to maintain their hold on the mind and soul of the human they are possessing.

Iron has always been known to have special properties when it comes to the occult world. I've never read any science about it, but who the hell is gonna capture the Lucky Charms guy or Bigfoot and cut on him to prove it kills faeries and monsters? All I need to know is that it works, and if you make your iron into 'cold iron' by leaving it out overnight under the light of a full moon, it does major physical damage to creatures that are otherwise immune to physical attacks.

You can riddle a shoggoth full of holes from a .357 and it will most likely just keep coming. Without cold iron you'll have to pretty much rip the things head off to put it down. With cold iron in your rounds you can pretty much kill 'em like you'd kill a man, at least most of the time. Never know what horrors you're gonna run into out there. After we got the shells engraved and re-armed, ole Conjure would light some incense, do a weird kind of dance, and spit perfectly good rum all over the shells. Something about the rum binds all the battle energy into the shells.

Seemed weird to me, but I suck down magic moonshine to fuel my hexin', so weird works just fine.

ROAD MUSIC

It's important to get your road music arranged, because this is the music you're going to live and die by. No kidding. We spend so much time on the road that we've gotta have some-thing better to listen to than Top 40 radio. As much as I loves me some Skynyrd and Johnny Cash, a man can only listen to so much classical music be-fore he's tired of even that. Be-sides, radio is mostly car commercials and talking heads these days anyway. Some folks have iPods, others have satellite radio, other old farts like myself have mixed tapes they've been listening to since the days cassettes replaced the 8 track, and hell, I might even have an 8 track stashed somewhere in Ronnie's shop.

The point is, you need music that gets your blood pumping, keeps you steady and awake, lifts your spirits, and that you don't mind blaring over your dead body, because chances are you'll die with the engine running.

CAJUN FOOD CURSES AND CURES

An astute observer of the culinary arts will likely take notice of the blatant omission of any kind of Cajun cooking, and that is intentional in the extreme. Southern cooking is a unique style, borne of the combination of desperation and ingenuity. Southern folks were having to make do with the cheapest cuts of domesticated meat or hunt and fish it themselves, substandard grains they could afford or scavenge, and whatever vegetables they could grow themselves or forage from the land. They cooked high calorie meals, heavy on the grease, and soak up every bit of it they could, with hard breads or bare hands. They were hard-bitten pioneers, farm laborers, and working folk of all manner of trades, and they needed every tiny calorie they could get.

Seriously, have you ever tried to eat a crawfish?

It ain't the beer-swillin' good time that the crawfish boils of city folk try to be. They're difficult and messy to harvest, tough to cook, and after all the work of peeling they usually just taste like mud.

Southern food also had its comfort side, and its own kind of class. We bring food to every event, be it a wedding or a funeral, and we pull out all the stops, because tomorrow might just not be here. Nobody is thinking about heart attacks, clogged arteries, or big bellies. Hell no, we're thinking about the dead, the recently hitched, hard work, and living for today. Cajun cooking is southern style for sure, but it has a dark side to it, one that I ain't willing to share the mechanical details of in this tome.

Let me put it this way, there's slayer cooking and there's sorcerer cooking, and while both of 'em are southern through and through, they have two very different functions.
Good slayer cooking ain't much different from regular southern cooking, beyond the fact that we empower what we're doing, and are careful to manage our ingredients, as they all have different attunements and energetic resonance. Communicating that, is really what this book is all about, and maybe telling a bit of my story in the process I suppose, but Cajun cooking is different.

Slayers cook for cleansing, for companionship, and for the simple joy of it, because even that joy is a weapon against the enemy. Cajun cooking is for sorcerers, plain and simple. Forget everything you think you know about Cajun cooking, turn off your Emeril Laggase and Anthony Boudrain TV shows, and avoid any of those faux high end restaurants in Nola. Sure as shit avoid any 'cajun food' chain restaurants. They've all been playing mockingbird chef, copying the recipes of hard men and women who have been fighting the darkness since before Louisiana was even an official territory.

The old sorcerers and slayers who came to the deep swamps and bayous now known as Louisiana faced down some of the nastiest things to ever crawl out of the deep dark down under, and what became known as Cajun cooking was their secret weapon. Booze alone wasn't enough to fuel the kind of magick that the sorcerers needed to go toe to toe with the nightmares that haunted those lands.

Remember, these folks were the hoodoo shamans and Celtic druids of their time. All immigrants, be that voluntary like the Scots and Irish, or in shackles like the Africans and Pacific Islanders. They stood in the face of that darkness and saw that it had seeped into the very land itself, such that the swamps themselves became the enemy. They were desperate, and someone, nobody knows who did it first, started making food using the creatures and plants of the land. They were transmuting that darkness into a power they could use against the darkness, fighting fire with fire as it were. Cajun food ain't for cleansing, it's for power, and that power is dark.

Sorcerers in those days would suck down a bowl of gumbo the way you or I would drain a bottle of whiskey, and then they'd drink the damn whiskey. No cleansing, only power, and though such tactics enabled them to beat back the nightmares, its forever left a stain on that kind of cooking. It's almost like the impact of that swampy Armageddon has echoed down through the years and to this day slayers avoid Cajun food.

About the only folks that you'll see cooking up a pot of gumbo or having themselves a crawfish boil are motherfucking sorcerers who know the truth, and everybody knows those shifty bastards live with one foot in the grave.

THE HOLE IS ALWAYS HUNGRY

When a slayer buys the farm, the understood tradition is funeral by fire, and there's a handful of reasons for it. The first being that fire has a cleansing power, it'll destroy what it's cleaning, which for us, is kind of the point. Slayers are carrying around a ton of darkness, from psychological to the spiritual, and going down to ashes is the best way to make sure all that shit gets dissipated and destroyed.

The second is that fire burial has always been the warrior's way to go out, from the Vikings burning their kind on ships or the Celts and native Americans building pyres on land and holding vigil while the flames did their work.

Granted, most slayer funerals I've witnessed are a touch less dignified than all that, as they're usually incorporated into actions taken by the survivors to cover their tracks. I remember the day that Dean Parker and Randy Logan went on their last run.

Me, Dean, and Randy had been piecing together a few murders, real nasty pieces of business in a little podunk town about thirty miles outside of Nashville. Being so close to the music capital of the world, we all assumed we'd be seeing Yellow Signs cropping up all over the place, but not a single one appeared.

Randy was a good old boy, a blues picker from down in my neck of the woods who had come to Nashville chasing his own dreams and nightmares. Nashville, being the place that it is, has always been a hotbed of mythos activity, specifically the followers of Narlythotep. He's the prophet and the crawling chaos, and he's always taking over this musician or that one and driving 'em towards his own dark ends. Randy figured that if he was in the thick of the music scene out there he might be able to head some of those nightmares off at the pass, as it were.

He started working in the 1970's as a guitar man, and has been doing it ever since, working for producers as a studio guitarist and filling in as a player for live shows when the acts needed an extra or a replacement. Being so tied into the music of the city, Randy could get close to musicians, he'd been in demand for so long that nearly anybody who's anybody, or who's gonna be somebody one day, ended up either playing alongside him or laying down tracks in his studio. Yessir, he owned his own joint, which honestly made him one of the few slayers I know who wasn't either living on the dodge or gluing pennies together to make nickels.

Randy had called me up about a week earlier to clue me in on some nefarious events unfolding in his backyard. The police had found the bodies of two musicians, real up and coming kids, who had been worked on something fierce. The way Randy puts it, these two kids were successful musicians in their own right, and had come together personally and professionally, started a new band, got a new album out, and right at the moment you'd think they were gonna break it big, they disappeared. It had been about two weeks since they'd turn-ed up missing, and from what he'd heard from his friend on the force these bodies were fresh kills.

Randy wasn't much younger than me, and couldn't walk without a cane and double leg-braces, so you can understand why he wanted some help. These days there are fewer and fewer of us carrying the torch, so I understand why he had to reach out all the way down to Louisiana. Now I'm getting up in years too, so I decided to cut hard east and stop in Mobile, Alabama, on my way north and picked up Dean Parker.

Now Dean was one of those young bucks who gives an old man some hope that we ain't all dying out. Dean was the son of John Parker. He was a gas station clerk when he needed to make a little cash, and medicine man of the local Choctaw people if anyone asked who he really was, which they didn't. Racism is still alive and well in the south. While Dean wasn't initially all that into his old man's spirituality, he picked up enough to be ready to lay down some whoop-ass when he met his first monster. Dean and his dad never talked about it, kept all stoic about it, but as I never heard mention of Dean's mother or why he had claw scars running from neck to navel, I figured it was the same kind of bad that puts all men on our path.

By the time we pulled into Nashville, with a truck load of guns, gasoline, and plenty of moonshine, there had been several unexplained fires in a small town roughly thirty miles out. Randy had left word that he'd meet us out there, and we met him at a little diner just off the highway. While Dean sucked down his breakfast and half of mine, I flipped through Randy's notes and got familiar with the case. There had been ten fires, some of them still burning, and it wouldn't be more than another hour before there were so many sheriff's deputies and fire department volunteers that we'd have trouble slip-ping away unnoticed. I used my pencil to trace a pattern using the fire locations on a printed map of town that Randy was thoughtful enough to have included. Right away I recognized the spiral, and managed to stop tracing the last of it as I realized what it was.

Who knows what would have happened if I'd finished tracing that pattern. Just looking at the thing was already making Dean push his plate away, and Lord knows that boy could have kept eating all day. I told Randy I figured we were dealing with a Devourer cult. If they'd already moved from murder to fires, it meant that they were nearing the apex of their development and were probably in the early stages of a grand summoning. The chance to nip this thing in the bud had long since passed, and we were going to have to hit them commando style. That's always how it is with cult investigations, to catch 'em early you've got to really put the investigation into overdrive and hope you get a lucky break. In those initial stages the cult is harder to root out, but once you find 'em its less of a fight. If you're late for the party then they'll be much easier to locate, hell, sometimes, like with these yahoos, they aren't even bothering to hide, because by then they're strong enough to take on just about anybody. They'll have local law enforcement and city officials either signed up as card carrying members or stitched up somewhere deep and dark. There's just no way to get it done clean, but the work still has to get done.

Now going in 'commando style' is a young man's game, and me'n Randy sure weren't spring chickens, but we figured it was get to it or go back home. Well, since we had Dean and all my daytime shows were in re-runs then, of course, we went in.

The Devourer is a simple god really; it's all in the guy's name. All that theological nonsense about how he's the sacred black hole, the great wyrm, the destroyer and the planet eater, well, you can leave that to the scholars and sorcerers. He's essentially one big mouth with an endless appetite. That makes the ritual site easy to find, just head for the middle of the whirlpool.

Even though I didn't finish drawing the symbol, it was easy to see where the center of the spiral was on the map, right smack in the middle of the town square. This was one of those old school small towns that was built around a central well back in the frontier days. We loaded up my truck with all of Randy's gear and started heading deeper into town. By then the sun was down, so to stay extra stealthy we kept the headlights off. Not like we needed them anyway, as it looked like more and more buildings were being set on fire as we plunged deeper into town. This had escalated so damn fast that as we got near the center we realized that the missing musicians hadn't been the beginning of the cult's process, it was more of a final push before the grand finale.

The place was lit up like Mardi Gras, with masked folks partying in the streets like it was the end of the world, and if they had their way it was about to be. At first, we thought we were seeing looters smashing storefronts and breaking into homes, but we quickly realized they were using the stuff they were lifting to start even more bonfires on the open roads and next to already burning buildings.

 Thankfully, the chaos and smoke allowed us to get pretty darn close to the town square before we parked the truck. Dean soaked three bandanas in bottled water and we tied those over our faces to help with all the smoke that was hanging heavy in the air. Practical man that I am, I had a few pairs of swimming goggles in the glove box. I'd been doing physical therapy at the YMCA back home, trying to work out some of the kinks in my joints, and I got tired of borrowing pairs all the time. Some would call it a stroke of luck that I'd have those handy, though guys like The Grin would call it being fondled by the fickle finger of fate.

The smoke and fire covered our approach as we did our best to blend in with the revelers, which was a hell of a lot easier than I'd have expected. Most of the partiers were wearing make-shift masks, some even bandanas, and a lot of 'em were armed, not as heavily as we were, but trust me, a guy in a carnival mask walking around with a can of beer in one hand and a claw hammer in the other is still armed.

Randy couldn't help but to chuckle as he broke out a hip flask of blended whiskey, infused with wormwood and splinters of rowan tree. Now that's a witch killer's drink if ever there was one. Between the three of us passing it back and forth, we drained it dry fast, but at 40% alcohol by volume and laden with mojo it had the three of us walking tall and feeling like badasses by the time we reached the square.

Cultists, I swear I'll never understand 'em.

The old town well had been covered in occult symbols and the kind of graffiti that made your brain itch. They'd built some kind of effigy of the Devourer using scrap wood, rope, and nails, then decorated it with about a dozen human jawbones, most of em looking pretty fresh. On either side of the well stood a musician, each one looking just as hip and ironic as they did in their press kits, holding their guitars and belting out tunes in a language that made my head spin. I felt the deepest urge to start partying with them myself, to drink, fuck, kill, loot, and burn right alongside 'em. Randy whispered through gritted teeth that it had to be the music, and he'd know.

Dean gasped, and we followed his gaze to see that one by one the participants were hurling themselves down the well. There was no pattern to it, just every now and then someone would walk away from whatever debauchery they were up to and take a header into the well. For a hot second I wondered where the cult leader high priest was, then remembered my lore, and recalled that in Devourer cults the first sacrifice was always the leader, whose body and soul kick started the whole party.

Man, you've can't begrudge 'em their dedication.

With that, I nodded at the boys to let 'em know it was time for the dust up. Dean whipped his assault rifle to his shoulder and started pounding rounds into the chest of the male musician, knocking him back step by step as he walked towards the well. Randy, old son of a gun, carried a lever action 30/30, and had put three holes in the female musician before she toppled over and started leaking black blood across the pavement. By the time I reached the well, the two musicians were down and the boys were reloading. I caught one believer in the chest with buckshot and then leaned my masterkey up against the effigy while I got to work.

We'd packed up all of my moonshine and cut up my last stash of canvas and crushed up a block of Styrofoam we found out behind the diner to make nine bootleg Molotov cocktails. I pulled the canvas plug from one and splashed it across the effigy, just to make sure it went up when I lit the rest. Dean and Randy were flanking me, standing about where the musicians had been, laying down suppressing fire.

Once the music stopped the revelers had taken notice damn fast. They seemed to be reacting in one of two ways. About a third of them were wailing and scratching their faces as they fell to their knees, while the rest had gotten real interested in taking us out. We knew we were exposed, so had to work fast, and the boys were burning through their ammo like it was Custer's last stand.

After I soaked the effigy, I lined up all the jars on the edge of the well and was about to light the first one when Randy screamed. Dean and I spun around and saw that all the black blood that had been leaking out of the female musician had defied gravity and was flowing up Randy's body. The shit was forcing itself into Randy's nose and mouth, causing him to convulse and make this bizarre growl in the back of his throat. I looked back at Dean to ask him if he was seeing what I was seeing, only to witness Dean begin twitching and spitting as the goo from the male musician he had killed worked its way inside him, too.

Now a younger slayer who ain't seen as much horror might not have reacted as fast as I did, but us old geezers have fought a lot of battles, seen a lot of good men and women die hard, and we know that in this fight there's no time for hesitation, no room for grief, until after the deed is done. I only had seconds before whatever transformation was happening to my friends was complete, so I ripped my bowie knife from its sheath and slammed it into Randy's neck. Folks these days seem to have forgotten how badass a good bowie knife can be. The heavy blade is shaped like a wedge, and if you keep it sharp, the knife can be used to chop and hew just as well as a hatchet.

My first swing brought Randy to his knees with his head flopping to one side, barely held on by his half-chopped neck bones. I grabbed him by the hair of his head, finished the job with a second chop and his head came away from the body. I stood up and turned around to face Dean, who had stopped twitching, but had his face pointed down at his feet. I dropped Randy's head in front of the well as Dean slowly looked up at me, and I could see in his hollow eyes that my friend was long gone, consumed by whatever darkness the cultists had called down into the bodies of those poor musicians.

I could tell by the wash of power slamming into me that whatever was inside Dean was throwing some major mojo at me, but thank God, I was still half-drunk from Randy's whiskey and none of it was able to take hold. The spell it was hissing just slid off my spirit like water off a duck's feathers. As the creature looked at me in surprise, I stepped forward and took its head off with the bowie knife in one clean stroke. I'd shoved the horror of the last few seconds to the back of my mind and did my best to focus on the task at hand. I knew that the cultists were closing in on all sides, and I didn't have more than a few seconds to make my play.

I pulled out my Zippo, a metal one I'd taken out of my dad's cabinet after he passed away. Though the metal was worn, it still had his initials etched into it. That lighter has never failed to spark for me, which is a kind of magic on its own. The lighter held true and flame jumped from it as soon as I thumbed the striker. I passed the flame over the effigy and it went up like a torch. A good thing, too, because a handful of revelers had reached the well. They were screaming and distract-ed by the burning effigy which bought me enough time to slap iron and drop three of the closest with my revolver before turning my attention to the shrine.

All of the shine had been brewed and infused with my particular brand of whoop-ass. I knew it was burning up more than just the wood and bone. I lit the first jar and chucked it down the well, sure as the rain that there wasn't anything left down there as whole-some as water. As I'd expected, the jar shattered against the side of the well and spewed the flaming Styrofoam and booze cocktail everywhere. The Styro-foam is the key ingredient of a good Molotov cocktail, and lots of folks don't know that. The Styrofoam makes the fire sticky, like napalm, so it burns hotter and longer. Nasty stuff really.

When I saw the dark mass of wet flesh, teeth, and tentacles that was hiding at the bottom of the well, I admit I couldn't help but to start screaming like a madman. I was equal parts screaming in victory and in terror, and I pitched three more cocktails down there in rapid successsion. The revelers thankfully all seemed to have succumbed to the wailing and face-scraping of their earlier companions, no doubt some fallout effect from me lighting up their boss and his statue.

Now when a slayer turns to the dark side, burning 'em won't work, because those who turn are usually the kind of sorcerer who ain't gonna let the pesky problem of not having a body stop him. Lead lined coffins is the best way to seal off the bad guys you can't fully kill, 'cause if you burn 'em their essence is sent to the out and above, just like a normal slayer, except these are sumbitches that you don't want getting spread anywhere. If you can't destroy 'em so hard that there's no coming back, then a lead box is the way to go. Ideally, use a water treated pine box, lined with plates of lead over all the major chakras, packed with salt and iron, wrapped in moontouched chains, and dumped in the darkest most inaccessible place you can find.

Obviously, I didn't have any of that for Dean and Randy, and neither of 'em were sorcerers anyway, though I was sure that whatever had worked its way inside them was the kind of darkness that wasn't going to die on its own. I could already see the goo starting to seep out of them, and I knew what I had to do.

I apologized to Randy and Dean, then quick as I could I threw their bodies and severed heads into the well. I winced as I heard their bodies impact wetly against the burning nightmare already down there, then I went ahead and hurled all but the last cocktail down the well after my friends. The fire was burning so hot that the stones around the top of the well were starting to smoke, as nothing burns hotter than fire fueled by combustibles and mojo.

I took up my masterkey and stepped away, taking care to blast a kneeling reveler out of my way as I moved. After I was a few paces back, I sent the last cocktail smashing into the base of the well, lighting the whole thing up, effigy and all. I didn't have to throw that last one, but goddamn it felt good, and so did gunning down the half dozen defenseless revelers on my way back to the truck.

I'm no hero, never said I was.

I drove back to the diner, and went inside, still armed and stinking of fire and blood. There weren't any customers left, just the waitress and the line cook, neither of whom looked me in the eye as when I walked past the register and into the kitchen. They stepped out of my way. The cook held his hands up and backed away from the grill; just stood there quietly, occasionally looking at the scared waitress as I cooked myself up a mess of eggs and hash. I was pretty sloppy about it too, on account of the fact that I was still cradling my masterkey in one hand, but I got the cooking done and slopped everything into a to-go container, along with some plastic utensils and a mess of napkins. I walked back out to the front counter and told the waitress to pour me a cup of coffee, black, and put a lid on it.

I threw a few bucks at the register and got out of there, food and coffee in hand. I got back in the truck and hit the gas, tearing ass out of town in the other direction as the lights and sirens of cops and firefighters came from the direction of Nashville.

Breakfast and black coffee never tasted so good.

BLACKWATER BLUES

There was a man who lived in a little Virginia town called Blackstone. His birth name was Kenneth Miller, though most people knew him as Saint Sebastian. Like most men and women who end up on the dark path, Kenneth started hearing voices, whispers coming from the shadowed marshes that surround the community of only a few thousand souls. Tale has it that something lived in the wild places around town, and folks called it the 'blackwater', which was exactly like it sounds. If it got on you it would flow in through your mouth, nose, ears, and everything else, and you would be different. A 'black-water man' would beat his wife, abuse his children and offer up family pets as sacrifices to things with unpronounceable names.

Assuming he (or she) hadn't been arrested for murder (which happens alarmingly often in Blackstone) the person would end up disappearing into the marshes. They'd just up and walk into the woods one day and never come back. Kenneth was changed by what he heard, the man who had once been a mild-mannered retail clerk at the local Wal-Mart got very, very angry. He star-ted grumbling to his co-workers, friends, family, and anyone else who would listen about the curse that plagued the town. At first, he was just a nuisance, until he started preaching and yelling sermons about the evil that had corrupted the town, that consumed its people one at a time. He railed against the blackwater, and defied it to come out into the light of day, to face him head on instead of lurking behind the eyes of hapless victims.

After a few weeks most people just wanted him to shut up and leave, be-cause nobody really believed in any of those stories, the blackwater people was just a tall tale they'd yell back at him. Crime statistics are just numbers and data for the fancy folk in city hall, they'd say. It didn't help that Kenneth, who had taken to calling himself Saint Sebastian, would more often than not be very drunk when he accosted the general public. He spent more than one evening sleeping it off in the old jail cells beneath the city courthouse. Once he started drinking, his sermons changed from warnings to demands for recognition, the angry man calling for the town to thank him for holding back the horrors.

He would screech about the radical reduction in murders and mayhem that the town had begun to enjoy since he began his self-proclaimed vigil. He began to tell anyone who would buy him a drink and listen for five minutes that he used the booze to cast spells on the nightmares that lived in the marsh, and that his drunken state kept him safe from the predations of the blackwater. He would claim that he was a warrior for good, and that only he could save the town of Blackstone from the evil that had taken root, then inevitably he would stumble away into the night, presumably to do battle with whatever terrors his broken mind had conjured to his eyes.

Local talk has it that one night, crazy old Saint Sebastian burned himself alive in his trailer home, which lay just outside the city proper. His family did not arrange a funeral for him. What remains they could sift from the ashes were interred in the local cemetery, along with a modest plaque paid for, reluctantly, by the city. It was in the mid-90's when I happened upon a small article in Drudgereport.com (a key news feed for slayers looking to find news that's not about celebrity pets or political election theatre).

According to what I read, a young woman had allegedly run away from home and was missing for three full days before turning up at the home of her boyfriend. The article was a bit vague on the details, but after reading between the lines, I gathered that it was the most gruesome crime scene in the town's recent memory. After killing her boyfriend the young woman is alleged to have gone into a gas station and drained four gallons of whole milk before hurling the attendant through the glass of the storefront. She disappeared into the night, and hasn't been seen since. This happened on the very night before a local folk legend, the afore mentioned Saint Sebastian, was found dead in the smoldering ruins of his home by firefighters responding to the 911 call.

Needless to say, even the Drudge-report had not linked the two cases, but after twenty minutes on Google, Facebook, and Twitter, I'd found out all I needed about this Saint Sebastian character to know I was dealing with a mythos incursion. Virginia was a long haul from my place in Louisiana, and despite the exhaustive list of allies in my little black notebook, not a one was able to head to VA to back me up.

Papa Proctor hadn't been seen or heard from in six months, Daniel Baxter was up to his eyeballs in cultists just outside Memphis and nobody else was answering their phones. The Grin couldn't even stop laughing at me long enough to say no. I was on my own and that's the most effective method I know for getting yourself perished, but hell I went, what else did I have to do that week? My garden was weeded, the goats were fed, and winter was months away, so no need to keep the water on.

I made the drive up to Blackstone, got myself a cheap motel, which happened to be right in the half-mile that counts as downtown, and started my search. I made up a likely story about being a construction contractor for a gig in Petersburg, a bigger town about thirty minutes up the road, layering in an excuse about being wary of the big city (which Petersburg ain't mind you). There was this curvy waitress at the local diner who smiled at me like she knew I was lying, but in general folks seemed to buy it, especially since I was willing to pick up a few rounds of beers for some of the local boys and play a mean game of pool.

While those kids were trying to win their forty dollars back, I kept the lite beer flowing and asked my questions. It took me one long night of boozing and pool to pull all the de-tails together, but it all told the story just as I've written above. The truth of it was written all over the faces of the friends I'd bought with cheap beer and billiards.

On my second day in town, more than a little hung over, I took the truck out to the late Saint Sebastian's place and had myself a look in person. There was crime tape everywhere, but I've never bothered honoring those false yellow lines and I wasn't about to start then. I had my suspicions that ole Saint Sebastian was one of the sad legion of what we call 'broken vessels', being folks who see the mythos, in one form or another, and are equally destroyed and empowered by that knowledge. Those folks who become slayers, for the most part, come through that awakening with their minds at least partially intact, but there's always those sad few whose sanity is shattered by what they see, what they hear, and the terrible truth of what they learn. For them the power is a burden, a curse if you will, and though plenty of 'em still fight the good fight (like poor old Saint

Sebastian), they are irreparably insane. It happens to all of us if we live long enough, but these broken vessels never stand a chance, and they're bat-shit crazy from the jump.

As I poked around the Saint's place I could see half-burned symbols that he'd warded his place with, using a mixture of his own blood and shit, which though effective don't have the finesse and (honestly) pleasing odor that more experienced wards entail (like essential oils, incense, smoke, and other things not so foul). Still, untrained folk use what they have, and body fluids and excretions (like semen or stool) are plenty effective in the magick, even if they have a cost in the temporal world (and polite society).

I found heaps of empty booze bottles and after tracking around the place, at least a dozen shallow graves that the cops missed. Damn deputies and forensic Nancies, they can't ever find the real clues. Too busy looking at bullet trajectories and wondering about time of death to look at the hard truth standing right in front of 'em.

There were fifteen graves in the property surrounding the burned down house, but only someone who looks for clues beyond the crime at hand is going to find that sort of thing. More often than not the crime you are investigating, however heinous and bloody, ain't the crime you're looking to prevent. There's crimes against humanity, and they're terrible sure as sure, but we're fighting an enemy that sees way past the limitations of mortality, flesh, and even time. You've got to learn how to see the horror behind the horror, and at the end of the day, that's what breaks a lot of folks who peer too deeply, be that by choice or circumstance.

Saint Sebastian, near as I can tell, put fifteen blackwater shoggoth in the ground with nothing more than a bottle of whiskey and the fire in his soul. He died before he could be shown just how big the battle fought really was, how important his vigil. That kind of shit makes me more mad than it does sad. Death and failure are part of the slayer's path, but doing so in ignorance, man, nothing pisses me off more than one of the good ones going down without knowing what it was all for. The bleak horror of it all must have been daunt-ing to a man like Kenneth Miller, but there he stood, swilling booze and slinging spells from his back porch at an enemy that never stopped coming.

It took me two days to track that girl down, and I did the deed extra hard for old Kenneth. I picked up her footprints at the burned out trailer and followed her back into those dark swamps, and believe me, brother, I didn't sleep a wink. Both nights out there I spent huddled up next to a campfire and a ring of torches burning all around me. I warded 'em with my blood, and yes, because I was out there all alone, I did use my own shit to spice up my defenses. Do any different and you'd have died out there in the night.

I found her waiting for me by an old homestead, in complete ruins other than the chimney and a root cellar. Half her face and body where burned to a crisp, but still she tried to tear me apart with the claws that sprouted from her fingers and the tentacles that she vomited out from her mouth, but I had come ready for a sideways kind of fight. I'd already put back half of my whiskey, and when I spoke the word of power she was held, struggling to move as her own mojo slowly tore through the invisible mess o' bindings I'd set down on her.

It took me all eight of my shotgun rounds to put her face down in the muck, and four good swings with my bowie knife to cut her head from her shoulders. After I'd empted my bottle of lighter fluid onto her body to set it ablaze, I sank to my knees and proceeded to drain the rest of the hooch I'd brought with me. I knew that I was going to need all the mojo I could get. I'm no sorcerer, so I had to drink myself almost to the point of passing out just to raise enough power. I coughed up the biggest spell of my life and pushed back on the horror within until I could close the Door of that root cellar.

The blackwater was bashing against it, trying to get out, but I warded the door with more of my own blood. I was near to passing out from the booze and the blood loss by the time I was done, but get it done I did. I warded that root cellar harder than anything I've ever encountered. I even left my own masterkey shotgun rigged just behind the door to take the head off the first person to open it again, to boot. I know that those cult types travel in packs, but at least I know they'll pay a price if ever they make the attempt.

I managed to make it back to town in about a day, having stumbled through the swamp all that night with my bowie knife in hand and ready for trouble that, thankfully, never came. I stumbled into the local diner smelling like blood, shit, booze, swamp, and fire, but hells bells that curvy waitress was happy to serve me up some steak and eggs before I even had to ask for it. You know what, I actually ended up taking that fine woman home with me, after a shower, a nap, and a chance meeting at the pool hall that evening. I'm not the sort to kiss and tell, I'm as good a gentleman as I can manage, but I tell you what, I think that gal knew I'd done her and the town some kinda favor by the way she put it to me once the lights were down and we got our clothes off.

A cynical bastard would make some crack about her being a 'woman of a certain age' and wearing the world's thickest beer goggles when I asked her back to my room, but I swear it wasn't like that. It makes me wonder though, honestly, if there are folks out there who may not be able to see the darkness, but can recognize the light in someone who fights it right off.

Sure would explain a lot, because she was a real pretty lady and I was a scarred up, ugly son of a bitch who got treated like a prince for one night.

HAIL TO THE KING BABY

There's more urban legends and tall tales about the King within slayer circles than even normal folk. He rose fast, and his music was intoxicating, as was the man himself. He was a great man, of that it's certain, but everything else is up for debate.

Some say he was one of the many faces of Narylathotep, pushing us down into the bloody quagmire of the Vietnam war, the violent unrest of the emerging civil rights movement, the burgeoning hippie culture, and the hungry maw of the central banking system. Those same folks claim that it was slayers who bushwhacked him in that bathroom, a couple of hardy boys doing the world a favor, and that many of the Elvis impersonators out there are trying to re-kindle that dark power. Others say the opposite, that Elvis was a voice in the darkness of that chaotic time, a moonshine swigging sorcerer with fancy moves and a microphone. Those folks will insist that he couldn't keep up the fight, and like most other sorcerers who burn that hot for that long, his life, mind, and body all started to crack under the pressure. They'll tell you that it was agents of Hastur that punched his ticket one night when they caught him with his pants down, literally.

I'm never sure, day to day, what I believe, though I do find it interesting that there really are two sides to Elvis. There's the down-home rock and roller from Memphis, singing from his heart and earning his stripes out there on the open road. Then there's what folks like to call 'Flying Elvis', the man in ridiculous costumes, playing Las Vegas lounges and showing off his wealth and privilege. It's clear that something changed, something beyond mere fame and riches, but whether it was Narylathotep calling the sheep to slaughter or a sorcerer burning out in the limelight, that's the question. Since I don't have any good answers, much as I don't want to, I avoid Elvis music, because there's no telling what kind of hoodoo might be tied into those tunes.

THE GREAT DEPRESSION

Dust storms caused a great darkness rise in the land. Folks took to wandering the wasteland, it was the slayers who found the foul thing out there in the dustbowl of Kansas and sent it packing. There aren't hardly any folks left who remember the Great Depression, and most of 'em are so stoic about it all, or just plain senile, that you can't get 'em to tell you much anyway. That being said, in the slayer underground there are still a few stories that make their way from camp to camp. The good old days of riding the rails and hiding in hobo camps are long gone, but they were heady days while they lasted.

THE LITE BEER CONSPIRACY

The truth is that lite beer is shit. It moves even less mojo than it does alcohol by volume, which ain't much anyway. Now, before you blow a gasket, let me explain. I've quaffed my fair share of cheap lite beer in my life. Hell, I've probably swilled barrels of the stuff in my years, but once you know the value of a good beer, you'll never touch the stuff again.
Now some slayer friends of mine think I'm a bit crazy for this, but I think that the rise to prominence of 'cheap American lite beer' was propagated by

one or more Mythos cults. They did this to weaken the magick of the south by hooking them on cheap mass-produced beer that wouldn't channel power the way all the small batch stuff could.

It gets you drunk on the cheap, but it fizzles away your power, and all you get is generation after generation of good ole boys who, instead of hexing the bad guys, just end up using that teenyweeny power boost to do the dumb shit stunts that all drunk rednecks are famous for. Here we are, supposed to be saving the world, and instead, we're jumping ditches with four wheelers, night racing our boats, and cow tipping.

SHOGGOTHS

The beasts that hunger for the flesh and souls of humankind are numerous and terrible. Some are borne of that old darkness, Leviathan, and come at us from the murky swamps, the lonely mountains, and the un-mapped forests that always wait at the end of old dirty roads.

They lurk at the edges of civilization, and reach through the cracks within our own walls. Some are star borne falling from above and beyond, come to walk our ground and sow their cosmic mischief.

Others still, are from far below, the deep ones, who rise from the ancient oceans like a nightmare of old sins now come due.

Talk around the campfire is that Shoggoth was the greatest of Cthulhu's minions, back during the old bad days. Over time, the word 'shoggoth' came to be the common word used to indicate creatures of the mythos. This is a great big weird world, and brother believe me, I've seen way more things that go bump in the night than just what the mythos has in store for us. However, at the end of the day those other 'creatures' are really just child's play, and since the myths and legends are mostly true, they're pretty damn easy to handle if you've read your Stoker and Shelly and carry a silver bullet or two.

Honestly, they don't even surface too much, as they don't want to tango with the mythos quite the way we slayers are wont to do. Creatures tend to be just as much a tasty snack for a shoggoth as a human, maybe even a little spicier. So there ain't much point in talking about all the other bad things that haunt us, because folks can handle 'em.

Shoggoth on the other hand, are pretty much immune to 'common folklore' type attacks and can turn aside your traditional defenses as if they don't exist. Hell, considering that for the most part the shoggoth are from a different reality anyway, it makes a bizzaro kind of sense that they'd be unaffected by our physics or our stories.

That being said, they sure as shit seem to be affected by rum glazed shot-gun rounds and a good smack from a hand axe. Not that your chances of survival are much above dead-meat if you ever have to fight one of these things without A) backup and B) a plan. I just barely survived my first encounter with one, and I got the drop on it, twice, and I'm still not totally sure I killed it for good. Might be there's a mess of tentacles and teeth our there still cursing my name and sniffing after my old farm truck.

Shoggoths can come in all shapes and sizes, but the main thing is that they don't appear in a vacuum. Shoggoths don't enter our world on their own. Someone, or something, has to summon them here. Now, once they put paw (or hoof, or belly, or tentacle, or worse) to ground they're here and ain't leaving unless they're commanded or killed. No two are the same, though all of them are damn powerful and hard as hell to kill. There are a few tricks here and there that folks have picked up on, like apple pie and shotguns, but there aren't too many surefire ways to battle these suckers. You have to make it up as you go and hope for the best, which is why I won't do it sober.

As I've said, there are tons of redneck cults and hillbilly clans who end up missing out on the Elder Gods and Outer Dark, and end up just worshipping the shoggoth themselves.

This is how most of the run-of-the-mill sacrifice cults get started. The folks start ma-king offerings to the shoggoth and discover that in its presence their magick seems to work better (which it does, something about the reality displacement field generated by most shoggoth). From there it's just a matter of time till their power-hungry inclinations and general unhinged nature (often fueled by poverty and drugs, which is a damn shame) that their appetite for sacrifice attracts the attention of either a high priest or a slayer.

The high priest, more than likely, will try to bring them into the fold of a larger and more embedded cult, turning them into foot soldiers for the core group (making them basically human shoggoth). Sometimes the high priest and the larger cult will just kill them off, for any number of reasons.

Suits me fine, since wiping them out is what any slayer would do, though if you can nab yourself a high priest and maybe crack open a bigger cult network, well… that's what we call winning the mythos lottery friend.

CROSSROADS ARE ALWAYS BLOODY

It's never a good idea to hang out at a crossroads, no matter what you believe. It never ends well. Then again, nothing much does in our line of work, but that's a foregone conclusion and we've accepted it. Most of us will make it part of our rounds to pass through any real deal crossroads in our chosen territory, or if we're making a cross country run, because such places are usually a good starting point for checking the pulse of the spiritual health of the area. If there's something hinky going down, the chances of getting your break in the case on a crossroads is pretty damn good.

I remember one time I was going solo from my place down in Shreveport up to a little spot in the Arkansas Ozarks to take some hexin' shine to this bush wizard we all called The Grin. He was one of the weirder slayers out there. Nobody knows what his real name is. He was maybe in his mid-thirties back then, so he hadn't been in the game all that long, but he was playing it hard.

While most of us rely on shotguns more than moonshine, there are some folks, who once they get a taste of that mojo, want more, and sure as sure, they are some serious badasses, but they lose their minds.

Don't get me wrong, it's good to have a full-on wizard in your corner, but more often than not, they lose touch with reality, and eventually they either burn out, get killed, or other slayers have to put 'em down for falling off the deep end.

Anyway, I was making the drive and The Grin insisted that I head the long way through south Arkansas instead of taking the bypass up through Oklahoma. I was driving through some out-of-the-way town and ended up at railroad crossing, which a lot of folks don't realize is not only a crossroads, but the biggest and baddest kind of crossroads.

The railroads, for the most part, follow the ley lines of energy that crisscross the whole country, that's why we call 'em 'the old straight track'. Railroads have some heavy medicine of their own, being so tied to not only the shipping of goods, but they carry a symbolic weight as the machines of bloody progress.

I stopped at the railway sign and had that feeling of creeping dread running up the back of my neck that usually spells trouble. I couldn't see anything from where I was, so figured I might as well step out. I pulled onto the shoulder and hopped out. I was careful to keep my .38 special in my pocket, since who knew who or what, was watching, and I certainly didn't want to be a stranger with a gun if I ran into one of these ticket-happy small town cops.

I did a quick check of the area and couldn't find anything, but damned if that dread wasn't still creeping and I knew I was gonna have to crack open a jar. I sucked down a hearty swig of the shine and leaned up against the hood of my truck, rolled myself a cigarette, and waited for the buzz to hit me.

I was about halfway through the smoke when the juice hit my system. Man, that pure grain alcohol really gets at you. I'd steeped fruit and spices in the jars, because The Grin likes the dreamsicle, precisely for the reason I was using it right then. That particular cocktail is spell crafted to let you see what is hidden, whether by its nature or by design. As the drink started kicking in, I could see these little red clouds of mist gathering near the drainage pipe right underneath the crossing. I couldn't believe I'd missed seeing that, and realized that someone had put up a shroud enchantment to prevent anyone from noticing it.

I filled my fist with the .38 and made my way across the ditch and down to the pipe. The mist parted as I walk-ed into it, my hex cutting through the shroud like it was nothing.

Yessir, I do make some damn fine shine.

Something in there smelled rotten as hell, so I tied my bandana around my face and peeked inside the pipe. Lord in Heaven, the moment I saw what was in there I knew I was gonna need some serious soul food. There was a woman's body in there, and yeah, yeah, I know there's always a body, but this one was messed up something fierce. Whatever dark worker had committed this atrocity had bound the woman's hands behind her back, tied her feet together, and blindfolded her. I've seen some bad things out there, and sadly that wouldn't have been enough to shake me up, but what got me was the fact that she'd been pierced by what looked like several dozen iron nails, big ones. Cold iron has a natural capacity for dissipating magical energy, but what a lot of people don't know is that you can use them to trap energy too.

One of the most effective ways to stop a ghost is to shoot that specter with a nail gun, which seems like a no brainer, but if you can't find the specter or it won't manifest, just find its bones and sink a nail into a few pieces. That will trap the specter inside its own bones, then you can salt and burn 'em like you normally would. The thing is, if the practitioner is powerful enough and they've got a few uninterrupted hours for the ritual, the soul of a living person can be trapped within their own body.

I know that sounds funky since we're all basically trapped in our flesh, but normal folks ain't bound to their bodies and when they die they just move on. If you've been bound you ain't going anywhere. It's big bad magick to do that to someone, because it's a bound living soul, so its energy regenerates, unlike a ghost which only has so much to go around. Some sick bastard had turned this woman into a soulbattery, her soul feeding the enchantment that had been laid out on the cross-roads. I didn't have the juice to see the complexity of the enchantment, I'm no Papa Proctor or The Grin, but that's the thing about being a slayer who ain't addicted to the mojo, I don't have to see, and I don't care to know.

I don't have to understand a thing to kick its ass.

I ran back to the truck and drove back the way I came and booked a room at the flophouse that passed for a motel on the edge of town. I didn't want to show my cards yet, and that's why I'm still alive. This old man is patient. I watched some Duck Dynasty and ate most of the cold fried chicken I'd packed for the trip. After some mindless TV and some soul food, I was feeling a ton better. Just being around that kind of bad juju will put the darkness on you, and that's why it's always good to pack some chow when you're on the job and don't know when you'll be able to get your next kitchen time.

I grabbed a shower, loaded my masterkey, and fixed myself a strong Tom Collins before stepping out into the night. I kept the shotgun in my duffel bag, along with my shovel, rope, salt, and bottle of lighter fluid. I had to stick to the shadows, didn't want to get spotted by some good Samaritan and get the cops out here before I could do my work. Being in the middle of rural Arkansas somebody might shoot first and call the cops after I was cold and dead.

I love the south, but folks certainly don't take kindly to trespassing.

After about thirty minutes I reached the crossroads, having come up through the wooded area that thankfully separated the crossing from the nearest row of houses. This town couldn't have a population of more than a thousand or so, but there were probably at least two or three police officers lurking out there, so I had to be careful.

The Tom Collins had given me that extra bit of supernatural luck that I knew I'd need to get here unseen, and so far the plan was working. I unslung the duffel bag when I reached the drain pipe and looped the rope through the corpse's hands and feet, then pulled hard and managed to pull it free from the pipe. It was wedged in there tight, but I'm a brawny guy and after awhile I got it done. I was feeling the pinprick of danger at the edge of my senses, and took a quick pull from my flask. In the flask was just plain old Jack Daniel's whiskey, which every slayer knows makes you stronger, faster, and harder to kill.

Whiskey Drunk is the most common hex out there, and every slayer keeps some on hand. Hexin' ain't for everyone, it requires some study, some practice, and there's always the risk that you'll get hooked on the power and earn yourself a one way ticket to epic glory and a gory end. Still, every slayers keeps some whiskey handy, as we need every advantage we can find. I was moving as fast as I could, and started pulling the iron nails from the woman's body. I could feel the dread creeping ever closer as I pulled each nail out. I had no idea what the spell was I was breaking, and I had no way of knowing who I was pissing off and what kind of retaliation they'd attempt, but there I was and Clifford Bartlett doesn't back down.

I pulled out forty-one nails by the time I was done, and all told it took me about five minutes. I didn't bother taking my rope back, and just left it wrapped around her. I dumped a handful of salt on the corpse just in case her soul was pissed off enough to try coming back as a specter, then poured the whole bottle of lighter fluid on her and threw a match on the body. I sprinted back into the woods once the fire kicked up, and I crouched down behind a tree to wait. I was cursing myself for not bringing a rifle on this trip, as I was going to have to come out of the cover of the trees to get a clean shot at whatever came calling, but hell, I guess that's why I carry the whiskey.

I waited and watched the body burn for another few minutes and then the police sirens started up and shortly there were two squad cars on the scene. The two cops were about as stereotypical as you could get, and I guess I'm a bit of a cliché myself, but that's how it goes. One was short, fat, older, and had an accent so thick even my Shreveport drawl would have seemed ur-bane. The other was young, tall, and looked like he spent all his spare time bench pressing tanks. The young guy put the fire out with an extinguisher from his trunk while the old guy watched.

They were poking around the body when a beat up Oldsmobile pulled up. Three men got out, all of 'em armed. The young guy shouted at them to leave the scene, but the older cop seemed to pull rank and tell the kid to back off. Now the old guy could have just been a good ole boy who wasn't all that much into police procedure, but these were three armed men approaching the scene of a grisly crime like they belonged there, and that didn't jive at all.

I was pissed I didn't bring more of the dreamsicle so that I could swig and see who was a cultist and who wasn't, but even if I had it with me I'd be too drunk to fight all that well, as I was already a bit fuzzy from the Tom Collins and all the whiskey. Maybe it was the Tom Collins giving me that last bit of luck before my liver soaked up all the mojo, but the battle lines were drawn when the young cop pulled his weapon and confronted the three armed men.

In the blink of an eye, it was one cop in a stand-off against the three strangers and the older cop, who was trying to talk the kid down. I slipped out of the tree line and ran to come up behind the three strangers. The whiskey was pounding in my head and I was moving faster than this busted old man should be able to move. I was in range just as the first of them noticed me. I shouted at the kid to find cover and started pumping rounds from the masterkey. I must have been a bit further away than I thought, as the buckshot fanned out, catching two of the strangers, who staggered as some of the shot pegged them, but neither fell down. I knew I was a dead man if I didn't get behind cover, but their car was still a few yards away, so I kept working the action and firing. I finally put two of them down, but just as I reached the car the third had raised his revolver and put a shot right into my chest.

I didn't get this old by being unprepared. I had my vest on, but that revolver was a .357 and kicked like a mule. The impact picked me up and threw me into the road, making me drop the shotgun and knocking the wind out of me. I heard more shots and people shouting, and prayed that the kid hadn't bit the dust. I was gasping and wheezing, but managed to roll behind the car as the last stranger emptied his revolver at me, thankfully missing every time. I pulled my .38 and raised it just in time to see the stranger leap up onto the trunk of the Oldsmobile and roar at me as his mouth distended to spill out a mass of black tentacles.

I screamed and emptied my revolver into the thing's face, then rolled over to vomit my guts out as the thing fell backwards in a spray of blood and black goo. I must have still been screaming and gasping when the kid rolled me over and slapped me back to reality. In the haze I managed to mumble that we had to take the thing's head off as I tried to get the trench shovel out of my duffel bag. The kid fired a few more shots into the shoggoth.

 I managed to get the shovel out and pull myself to my feet. I tried to walk to it, but fell down again, realizing that my sternum might have been cracked by the gunshot. I wheezed for the kid to take the shovel and hack the thing's head off as it thrashed on the ground, grievously wounded, but slowly recovering. The cop was in shock, but after I forced him to suck down a few swallows of whiskey he took the shovel and got to work. I looked around and saw that the kid must have shot the older cop, who was face down in a pool of blood near the burned corpse.

After the shoggoth was dead, I got the kid to swig some more whiskey to calm his nerves, then coached him on a story to feed to the sheriff's department and state troopers that were likely to be next in line to respond. Then I told him to meet me at the town diner as soon as he could get free and that I'd explain everything.

He managed to pass it off as a murder cover-up gone awry. The three strangers had been locals, so he was able to paint a picture of himself and the older cop catching these three guys in the act of burning the body of their victim.

I have to hand it to him, later, when we met at the diner he took it pretty well. I had him wolf down a chicken fried steak dinner, follow it up with some peach cobbler and a few cups of strong coffee.

Then I gave him the speech.

You know the one.

The speech where a slayer tells you about the Mythos, about looking into the face of the abyss, and how you're in it now and there's no going back.

I still wheeze every now and then, that shot to the sternum never healed quite right, but The Grin got his hexin' shine, we busted up some kinda rotten plot, took down a shoggoth, and now there's at least one good cop in south Arkansas who's keen on the Mythos.

THE SIDEWAYS REALM

There is more to this world than what is dreamt of by man. There is something more terrible and solid than our physics can illustrate waiting in the darkness between the stars. There are places where the angles are all wrong. There is a world behind the world.

Meet me in the alleyway.

Go to the place where the railroad tracks end.

Pass through the door at the bottom of the earth.

Count the bricks and turn around three times.

Follow a dirty road into the bayou, find the house full of sticks and you're in Carcossa now.

Dive down deep beneath the river dam into the flooded town that is R'yleth.

Cold Kadath is up in the mountains, just seek out the place where the law don't go and the children all look the same.

Anywhere there be the cults of evil men, such places will rise. It has all been said a thousand times a thousand ways.

Being a slayer has its freedoms, in that we can do as we must, we are not bound by the laws of the common man, though such makes us enemies of those laws, and them as enforces 'em.

Cops generally ain't our friends, unless they're one of us. That being said, every now and then you'll find a good egg. Let me tell you, having a friend on the force will fast track your casework. We can use the internet and public records just like anybody, but a cop has access to databases and files that civilians like you and me can never get our hands on. We can do a lot on our own, and most of the time that's about all we can do, but every now and then, a friend on the force can make a world of difference.

The thing about cops is that they see patterns, they're trained to see them, whereas most of us just pick it up along the way. There is a usefulness to that kind of trained precision, and it complements our 'street smarts' very well. You know cult activity when you see it, you can sense the touch of the mythos on a crime scene or an emerging situation. The cop can see the devil in the details, as it were, and precisely because he ain't looking for the devil is why the cop will usually find him (or her, or IT most likely) before you do. However, there's one thing all cops miss, one kind of wall they walk right into, or more appropriately, a door they don't know they've walked through until after it's too late.

See, the thing is, cultists, for the most part, have seen things that no man was meant to see and come away unchanged and unscathed. At the end of the day, all who have contact with the Mythos are damaged goods, but cultists have it in spades. When a man is faced with that deep darkness he has to fight it or embrace it, else be destroyed by it. Most folks, them as ain't turned irreparably insane or just plain die, choose to embrace it. Their insignificant human minds can't comprehend what they've seen, and the tiny lanterns of their human souls are tarnished by the presence of that deep dark, that Otherness.

The cultist, often with little guidance by their leadership, will begin to craft the world around them to resemble the world that pulses within them. The longer they carry on the more complex and powerful their local environment can become. There's a reason that the bayous of Louisiana are bad-land country, because the Cult of the Yellow Sign and the servants of the King have run amok in those swamps for generation after generation.

Their realm of Carcossa extends across much of the state, but here's the thing, it's not really here. Reality is a multi-verse, and there are layers upon layers upon layers of perception, and that's just what we know about with our pitiful human mathematics and spiritual understanding.

What these cult folk create is what me, and most slayers, call 'the sideways realm', mostly because to all of your senses it appears to be the 'real world'. It doesn't seem, at first, like you've crossed over from the 'real world', except for the subtle differences (in addition to the obvious ones). The obvious signs that you've crossed, is that the whole area will be filled with signs of the mythos. Symbols painted on walls, little trinkets and magick talismans hung or set about everywhere, or even some meth-head cackling that you're in his world now, that's the obvious stuff.

What's not so obvious is how shit works there. It's a lot like a movie, or a story, like a living legend. It's like the whole world becomes a big melodrama, and everything is amped up be-yond realistic limits. People say and do epic shit, sometimes for good and sometimes for bad. The worst acts of cruelty and debauchery are matched by relentless heroism and determined vengeance. Guns are less accurate in general, but more accurate when the moment depends on it. Blades are more effective, and it sure seems easier to sneak around.

General theory holds that the side-ways realm is another layer of reality that is closest to ours, like a little bubble realm within our own. A pimple of alternate reality on the face of our world.

If you can't engage the cultists away from their 'local haunts' then you are most likely going to have to go in after them, and that's when you'll find yourself in the sideways realm. Plenty of the stories I've told in this book start off in this world, but before it's all over and the blood is done spilling me and the folks have crossed over into their world, into the side-ways realm. It's a risky business friend, because while our heroism is amplified, so is their bad mojo and crazy badassery.

Chasing a redneck junkie into the sewers he frequents for his nefarious deeds is a bad enough situation as it is, but if he has been building altars, casting spells, and making offerings to the Skin Eater then you're stepping into the Labyrinth of Kesh and probably going to have to fight something way worse than one redneck with a drug problem.

This is another reason we slayers like to start fires and blast things with homemade dynamite. You've got to destroy the realm just as much as you've got to kill the cultist, because even though the realm was spawned by the cultist, that realm can persist on its own, even self-propagate. As I've said before, these backwoods hillbillies usually end up worshipping such places, and the beasts that lurk in and around them. Whole new cults can spring up twenty years after you gun down the original group just because you didn't completely destroy the sideways realm that had sprung up around them. All it takes is a curious and easily influenced someone to stumble upon a talisman, a book, or some graffiti, and that chance encounter will lead them into the realm, where they'll face the deep darkness, and the cycle will start all over again.

THE BAD OLD DAYS

I had me a wife once, a son too, and a few dogs, all on twelve acres of good black dirt in the Arkansas river delta. I lived in a little town called DeValls Bluff, and a more cursed and blighted place you'll never set your eyes on far as I'm concerned. I met Beatrice Walker when I was sixteen, which is so far in the past that I ain't even gonna tell you what year, you'd call bullshit considering the fact that I'm still spry enough to put shotgun and moonshine to the Mythos.

Suffice it to say, we had the storybook southern situation, where I meet her when we was young, we married right out of high school, had ourselves a kid, moved out of our small town to another small town intent on making our own way. I had been working as a farm-hand and mechanic since I was a kid, and honestly, my daddy was good about teaching me about money, so when we decided to strike out on our own I had the scratch to buy some acres and a travel trailer. We stayed in the travel trailer for a year or so while I built the house, and I was done just in time to bring home my first and only son.

I'd picked up plenty of odd jobs around town that year, and folks knew me as a hard working man who could do everything from walking rice levies to fixing engines to tending livestock. With my extra cash I bought a handful of pigs and got into the hog business. I have to chuckle at bit in my old age that I chose pig farming, since it all started with the pigs. I'd been doing okay with raising pigs, and sold enough pork to cover the bills and squirrel away some cash for that inevitable rainy day that seems to keep southern folk always living hand to mouth. That rainy day is coming for all of us, my friend.

We lived right at the edge of town, just maybe a mile down some gravel roads, with our property line nestled right up against the Wattensaw Game Preserve, which is about eighteen thousand acres of shitty swamp and a few oxbow lakes. Unless it was hunting season there wasn't much traffic through there other than the handful of farmers who had land lease out there or the various smugglers, rum-runners, and meth cookers who used the remote vastness as a place for their dirty dealings.

Most folks gave my place a wide berth, especially since they knew that I wouldn't know about a thing that went on or mention any traffic I might see as long as every month or so there was a little cash or a jar or two of the good stuff in the old bucket I kept hanging from a post at the front of the driveway. It was a good life, while it lasted. My boy was six years old, growing like a weed, when the thing came out of the swamp and tore apart the little life I'd built.

Back in those days I was as ignorant as any other good ole boy, so when I woke up around 3 a.m. to the screams of pigs, I grabbed my double-barreled shotgun and went out there looking for a fight. Now that I know better, I'd have had a hefty pull from the jar, set Beatrice to making eggs and biscuits and put iron and salt in my shells before setting foot outside. As it was, I assumed wild dogs had muzzled their way into the pen. Coyotes and wild dogs get a bad rap, as they don't cause near the damage folks claim they do, but a starving animal is capable of great and terrible things.

As I was running past the old travel trailer and towards the pen, I could hear the sound of tearing meat and the deep wet crack of bones being broken. I knew this was no wild dog attack, though what it was I could never have imagined. I figured maybe one of the meth cookers or maybe some of their competition had it in their head to scare me of my property by slaughtering my livelihood. It was the only thing I could think of as the screaming continued and I came up on the other side of the pen. I rushed around the corner and raised my shotgun, ready to shoot me some pig killers, and found myself face to face with a shoggoth.

Now, as you know, the shoggoth can come in all manner of shapes and sizes, some of 'em looking half-way human and others being not much more than a ball of tentacles and teeth. This one was something like a circular mouth attach-ed to the body of a man, but the arms and legs all had extra joints that bent in ways that made me sick to my sto-mach. Out of its elbows and knees there were these thin tentacles that moved like whips, the ends of them tipped with a hook or barb that ripped through the flesh of the pigs as the creature rampaged around the pen.

Lord forgive me, all I could do was stand there like a drooling idiot as the thing killed the last of my pigs. It was like my mind had seized up as hard as my muscles, and I was frozen in place. The shoggoth have that effect on a man, even if it ain't his first time to witness them, which is a big part of why we gotta do our job half-drunk most of the time. All I seemed to be able to focus on was the pig blood dripping from the thing's gaping maw and the scratchy wheeze that sounded at first like maybe it was laughter.

It was still for a moment, both of us just standing there looking at each other, and then it started flowing towards me. I still couldn't move, even though my instincts were shouting at me to move my ass, it just wasn't happening. It came right up to me, its' hot breath stinking like pigs and shit and death, and that's when I heard my son scream.

Nothing else in this world will motivate a man towards violence like the sound of his child in peril. It was like all the clouds in my mind faded away, and my frozen muscles burned with adrenaline. I swept the shotgun upwards and stuffed the barrel into the fold of flesh right under the creature's mouth and emptied both barrels into that son of a bitch. I don't know if the ichor that splattered all over me and the pen was blood or something more foul, but a good half of what passed was the thing's head disappearing in a cloud of fire and gore. The thing was knocked onto its' back and was writhing around making that wheezing sound as it flopp-ed around on the ground.

I turned around and started sprinting back towards the house, doing my best to reload the shotgun as I went. I'm better at it these days, but that night I dropped at least three shells before I could get the damn thing locked and loaded. I came up the porch in a dead run and kicked my own door open, shouldering it aside as it swung back from the force of my blow. I shouted for my boy as I moved deeper into the house. When I didn't hear him again I called out for Beatrice, and still nothing back. I moved through the living room into the kitchen, then down the hall to my boy's bedroom. The door was open and what I found inside ain't something I'm going to describe to you here, but if you're reading this book in the first place then you've known pain and you've known loss.

I heard the sound of a truck engine coughing itself to life, and after a last look inside the boy's room, I rushed out the backdoor to check it out. I came out of the house to see a truck pulling out of the driveway, and in the back were two men standing in the bed, with my wife trussed up and laying between 'em. They took a shot at me when I came out, but I was lucky enough to stumble down the first step of the back porch and fell off without getting hit. I wasn't gonna shoot and risk hitting my wife. At that range I wasn't going to do much than spread shot around. They spun out of the driveway and took a hard left, headlights pointed towards Wattensaw as they hit the gas and spit gravel.

I hauled myself up and ran to my truck, praying to the Lord above that I'd left my keys on the dashboard. My luck held out. I got the truck fired up and put the pedal to the metal. As I was speeding towards the driveway that bastard shoggoth came running around the corner of the house. I didn't have time to slow down, and I figured it was like meeting a deer in the road, when you're going too fast you don't swerve, you just keep it steady. Better the deer than you is the common wisdom, and after growing up on the back roads of Arkansas, I had that deeply ingrained, so when the thing came around the corner I sped up and held the wheel steady. It was already missing half its head, so it wasn't moving too well anyway, though still way faster than it should with only half a damn head.

I plowed through it and I'll admit that I let out a good old fashioned rebel yell when I felt its bones crunch under my wheels as I kept on going. I hit the gravel at speed, but I'd been driving on these kind of roads my whole life, so I was ready for the flow of the road, and managed not to bottom out on the rocks.

 I could still see the truck's lights ahead of me, and as they drew near I could tell I was going easily twice their speed. Apparently they didn't want to get away as bad as I wanted to catch up. The driver tried to lose me a few times by making hard turns down a few of the shittier roads, hoping that I'd lose control and ram into the swamp, but I kept to the wheel and got closer and closer.

I'm no genius, but this was my home, and after a few more turns I figured they were heading for the White River, which has a few boat slips not far from where we were. That was the only piece of civilization out this way, and they sure seemed like they'd rather get there than turn around and fight me. I didn't want to have to mess with both guys and the driver when we stopped, especially if they had friends on that boat I imagined they were running for, so I pushed my luck again and pulled alongside them. My whole driver's side of the truck was grinding through the muddy ditch that passed for a shoulder on these single lane back roads, but it was enough to get me smashing into the side of their truck.

Now, I was no gunslinger back in those days, but they'd murdered my son, had their pet kill my pigs, and kid-napped my wife, so there was no doubt in my mind that it was gonna get down to killing. I lifted the shotgun and pulled the trigger, blasting out the passenger window of my own truck and knocking one of the guys off his feet with buckshot, sending his bloody corpse sailing into the darkness of the swamp. I only had one shot left, so I had to make it count, but I was forced to drop the shotgun when the other guy returned fire. Most of the buckshot pinged off the metal of the truck frame, bit into the dashboard, or chewed up the seat, but some pellets hit me in the thigh and a few dug into my shoulder.

I did my best not to pass out from the blood and the pain, but there was no way I was gonna be able to pick up my gun with my right hand. I could see lights ahead and knew that it was the running lights of the boat I'd been right about. I was out of time and out of options, so cranked my wheel and drove the front of my truck into the side of theirs as hard as I could and kept the pressure on. The driver tried pumping the brakes, but must've also instinctively turned his wheel because the truck slid on the loose gravel, letting me ram into their truck in a perfect t-bone. I kept my foot on the gas and prayed as we reached the boat slip. Someone was shooting at me. I don't remember whether it was the guy in the back, the driver, or the boatman, but somebody was turning my truck into Swiss cheese and at least one of those rounds hit my chest like a punch that took my breath away.

By then I'd gone blood simple. The only thought in my mind was smashing their truck into the boat, which, by God, I did. The boat wasn't much, just a glorified flat-bottom really, room enough for a handful of folks and some supplies, a river fishing boat. Definitely not something that could handle the impact of two trucks.

I passed out for a little while after the impact, not sure how long, maybe a minute or so, but the smell of cooking meat woke me up. I grabbed my shot-gun and stumbled out of the passenger side of my truck; the driver's side was bent closed, and stood gazing at what I'd wrought.

The boat was already half-sunk, a truck sized hole in it, and there was a body floating out there, presumably the boatman. My truck was pretty beat up and shot full of holes, but nothing like the twisted and burning heap that was the truck I'd hit.

I looked in the truck bed and was happy to see the guy's corpse, but there was no sign of my wife. That's when I noticed all of the blood smeared on the ground, leading away from the wreckage. I followed it around to the back of my truck and looked up, seeing the truck driver dragging the body of my wife down the road.

I limped my way towards them, shouting for him to stop and firing a warning shot into the air. He came up short and turned to reveal that he was just as messed up as I was, bleeding from a dozen wounds and bruising up bad. I could tell then, that my wife was already dead, splinters from the boat having shredded her chest and no doubt punching into her lungs and heart.

The man was babbling something about recovering their shoggoth's baby, about how it had visited her in the night without my knowing. How there was a baby inside her they'd been sent to recover.

It's only now, in my old age, that I can really remember what he was saying, and even then it's all fuzzy. Back then, I wasn't listening, just walking towards him. My shotgun was empty, but I didn't bother reloading it as I pull-ed out my skinning knife.

He took a long time to die, babbling on and on about my wife and the baby and how Hastur was gonna eat my soul.

I spent the night walking back, my wife's body in my arms. I burned my house down the next day, with my wife and son inside.

I had no idea at the time, that this was the beginning of the nightmare, and not the end.

PREACHING THAT GOSPEL

This here is a copy of a manuscript that has been circulating around the slayer resistance since the Civil War. I ain't saying that me or anyone I've ever known has met one of these return-ed dark beings, or seen Nekhat face to face. What I do know is, sorcerers whisper that much of our power, especially our hexin, comes from the shatter-ed pieces of gods, monster, and god-like men who have fallen from the realms above and below.
This book tells us all about the dark gods, their followers, and according to many of the academics in our world, it helps us see our place in the greater cosmos. Plenty of insights into what the cultists are up to, and

a ton of info about the hurt locker they've got their minds set on opening.

If there was a bedtime story about where slayers go when they die, this is it, and it's no picnic. Even the after-life is a rotten mess of tentacles and cultists and the ding dang Elder Gods. I've never met one of the returned souls, but I know we've got some allies out there, and they've showed us a thing or two, given us some hope, and a way to fight. We turn the darkness against itself, tap into that little slice of evil in all of us and let it loose on the bad guys and their beasts.

The first slayers to hold the gospel were able to find that dark spark, mix it with the booze of the day, and turn it into hexin'. They gave Hastur his first bloody nose back in those days and it's been a fist-fight ever since. The talk is that one day Nekhat is gonna show back up and make things even harder for us, siding up with the likes of Narlythotep and Hastur and stinking up the place. Until then we keep fighting the good fight and get ready as best we can. It ain't pretty and it ain't clean, but it's what we have.

So here you go.

THE GOSPEL OF THE TENTACLE

As taught by Nekhat of the Pallid Mask, Who once dreamt upon the shores of dread Carcossa

REALITY IS A PRISON

There is a place that surrounds the earth from all possible positions, lying between this world and the next. It is a place that was built by unknown beings to protect us from the Dark. It is known by those of us who suffer within its boundaries as the Construct. During my time in this most horrific of realms as a disciple of Nekhat, I was shown a copy of the Necronomicon, known to my kind as the Book of the Black Earth.

What you hold is that vile book, paired with my own scribblings from within the Construct. The Old Ones are coming and there is no stopping them. Such monstrosities as the Construct can only delay them for a short while. Should you choose to use this book to battle their coming or hasten their return…that I leave unto you. The Pall-id Mask has been lost, and whomsoever finds it shall become the King in Yellow and stand upon the Earth, and with this Gospel shall have the power to choose Light or Dark, and thus the fate of all.

THE OLD ONES AND THEIR SPAWN

The Old Ones were, the Old Ones are, and the Old Ones shall be.

From the dark stars They came ere man was born, unseen and loathsome They descended to primal earth.

Beneath the oceans They brooded while ages passed, till seas gave up the land, whereupon They swarmed forth in Their multitudes and darkness ruled the Earth.
At the frozen poles They raised mighty cities, and upon high places they

created temples for Those whom nature owns not and the Gods of Earth have cursed.

The spawn of the Old Ones covered the Earth, and Their children endured throughout the ages. They are the giants of the earth, the Nephilim, as called by the prophets of men.

They have walked amidst the stars and They have walked the Earth. Mountains, deserts, and seas all bear their Mark.

Wantonly, the Old Ones trod the ways of darkness and Their blasphemies were great upon the Earth; all creation bowed beneath Their might and knew Them for Their wickedness.

The Elder Lords opened Their eyes and beheld the abominations of Those that ravaged the Earth. In Their wrath They set their hand against the Old Ones, staying Them in the midst of Their iniquity.

The Elder Lords cast Them forth from the Earth to the Void beyond the planes where chaos reigns and form does not abide. The Elder Lords set

Their seal upon the Gateway and the power of the Old Ones prevails not against its might.

Loathsome Cthulhu rose then from the deeps and raged with great fury against the Guardians. The Elder Lords bound his venomous claws with potent spells and sealed him up within the depths of the sea wherein beneath the waves he shall sleep death's dream until the end of the Aeon.

Beyond the Gate dwell now the Old Ones; not in the spaces known unto men, but in the angles betwixt them. Outside Earth's plane They linger and ever await the time of Their return; for the Earth has known Them and shall know Them in the time to come.

After day cometh night; man's day shall pass, and They shall rule where They once ruled. As foulness you shall know them and Their accursedness shall stain the Earth.

THE DARK

In a time before the Light, there was only darkness. In this time, reality was ruled by many races of vile, corrupt, and evil creatures. Some took the form of many slithering beasts, others choose to have no form at all, and were content to exist as swirling eddies within the darkness.

These great beasts lived in a state of constant bloodshed, locked in an eternity of violence and chaos. There was no change, no evolution, only stagnant and perpetual carnage. The strong preyed upon the weak, and the weak banded together to bring down the strong, then promptly turned on each other.

 Existence was nothing more than an orgy of blood and madness.

THE CREATORS AND THE STORY OF LIGHT

No one knows how, or when, the change occurred, but at some point a group of beings came into existence and brought with them the Light. Some theorize that these beings were actually creatures of the dark that grew tired of the endless bloodshed and created the Light as a way to escape from the

Dark. Others think that they were not creatures of the Dark, but that they were different creatures entirely and they created Light to combat the darkness.

All that is known, without doubt, is that these creatures came to primordial Earth and created the Light. They drove out the creatures of the Dark and allowed life a chance to change, grow, and evolve. There was no darkness or corruption on Earth, there was no evil and no strife. The bringers of the Light must have known that the Dark would seek out the Light, like moths to a flame, and try to destroy it, for they built what has come to be known by its inhabitants as the Construct. Then, as suddenly and mysteriously as they had appeared, the Lightbringers vanish-ed into the depths of the un-known.

THE CONSTRUCT

The Construct is an invisible shield realm that surrounds Earth on all planes of existence. It is a literal maze of halls, rooms, and archways.

There are multitudes of domed rooms, staircases, passageways, secret doors, and many other architecturally convoluted structures. The purpose of the Construct is to trap and destroy creatures from the Dark when they try to pass through it and get at the Light. Most of these dark forces are stopped by the strength and magnitude of the Construct's barriers, but the few who get inside the Construct do not get to the other side alive. Once inside the Construct, they are in constant danger of getting lost in the complicated maze or being destroyed by the many hidden death machines within the Construct it-self. There are multitudes of booby-traps, lethal puzzle rooms, false floors, and passive aggressive torture and execution devices everywhere in the Construct. The Construct was brutally efficient and nothing escaped it through for ages.

Until Leviathan.

LEVIATHAN

Leviathan was the largest and most powerful creature of the Dark to attempt to reach the Light. Leviathan was so powerful that the barriers of the Construct buckled under its force and it gained entry to the interior of the Construct. The Construct's death machines were not able to stop Leviathan and it forced its way through the other side of the Construct. Leviathan ripped its way out of the Construct and was torn asunder even as it entered the Light. It had used up too much power defeating the Construct and was too weak and wounded to hold itself together while in the presence of the Light.

Leviathan's remains fell to the uncorrupted Earth in many pieces, shards of Leviathan's tainted essence falling over the entire expanse of the Light. Darkness had found its way into the Light. On Earth these shards of essence melded with the world, corrupt-ting anything they came in contact with. Horrible beasts roared in the night, crops failed, water became poisoned, disease spread, and evil men began to walk the Earth.

HELL IS BORN

It was shortly after Leviathan's assault that a very important aspect of the Construct became apparent. When the taint that resided within the Light was released; blighted land being blessed, beasts being slain, evil humans dying, the tainted essence went back into the Construct to be destroyed and expelled back into the Dark.

When something of the Light expired, it was reintegrated into the Light. When untainted humans died their souls were recycled back into the Light from whence they came. However, when a tainted human died, their soul did not go into the Light, it went to the Construct.

These tainted human souls suddenly found themselves embodied in the Construct. They could move, act, and feel pain. In the Construct their souls manifested in seemingly physical forms. These unfortunate souls would usually not survive long against the

death machines within the Construct. Those that managed to elude death became predators in their own right, and souls were destroyed in droves. When they were destroyed in the Construct, the taint would leave their spiritual bodies as a black mist called Corpus, that seeped from their bodily orifices and was sucked out into the Dark by the Construct. What was left of their soul once the taint was gone became assimilated into the material makeup of the Construct. The inhabitants of the Construct believe that is why the walls sometimes moan and weapons seem to whisper.
If Leviathan's taint had been the only source of the Dark on Earth then the Construct would have eventually been able to force all of the darkness out of the Light. Unfortunately, this was not the case.

While Leviathan's taint resided in many places, once it was released, there was no more taint present. Only individual beasts and landscapes would be tainted by Leviathan's touch; for humanity things were dreadfully worse.

For some unknown reason, humans with tainted souls were able to spread their corruption and cause other souls to become tainted, not with Leviathan's essence, but their own. Humanity's corruption started with Leviathan, but something already present in humans had been awakened. Humanity began to generate its own unique darkness. The ranks of the Construct's population began to swell as the tainted souls of humanity became legion as civilization progressed ever onwards.

RAISE UP THE STONES

To form the Gate through which They from the Outer Void might manifest, thou must set up the stones in the elevenfold configuration under the Pyramid of Heaven.

First, thou shall raise up the four cardinal stones and these shall mark the direction of the four winds as they howl through their seasons.

To the North, set the stone of Great Coldness that shall form the Gate of the winter-wind, engraving thereupon the sigil of the Earth-Bull.

In the South, thou shalt raise a stone of fierce-heat, through which the summer winds blows and make upon the stone the mark of the Lion-serpent.

The stone of whirling-air shall be set in the East where the first equinox rises and shall be graven with the sign of he that bears the waters.

The Gate of Rushing Torrents thou cause to beat the west most inner point where the sun dies in the evening and the cycle of night returns. Emblazon the stone with the character of the Scorpion whose tail reaches unto the stars.

Set thou the seven stones of Those That Wander the Heavens, without the inner four and through their diverse influences shall the focus of power be established.

In the North beyond the stone of Great Coldness set the first the stone of Saturn at a space of three paces. This being done, proceed thou widdershins placing at like distances apart the stones of Jupiter, Mercury, Mars, Venus, Sul and Luna marking each with their rightful sign.

At the center of the so completed configuration, set the Alter of the Great Old Ones and seal it with the symbol of Yog-Sothoth and the mighty Names of Azathoth, Cthulhu, Hastur, Shub-Niggurath and Nyarlathotep.

The stones shall be the Gates through which thou shalt call Them forth from Outside man's time and space.

Entreat the of the stones by night and when the Moon decreases in her light, turning thy face to the direction of Their coming, speaking the words and making the gestures that brings forth the Old Ones and causes Them to walk once more the Earth.

NEKHAT

The passage of time is hard to track in the Construct, but at some point, a group of tainted souls left the known parts of the Construct vowing to find the truth. They were a group of souls that had once been scientists, theologians and philosophers, bent upon discovering the nature of their situation in this strange and deadly place, but they disappeared into the Construct and were forgotten.

Sometime later, one of the group, a woman, emerged from the wilderness of the Construct. At first, many were eager to learn what discoveries had been made and how she had survived, but soon they grew fearful. She was not the same creature that had left them be-fore, she was something different. She began to destroy her previous enemies with powers beyond imagination, after which she turned upon many others, seemingly at random.

Most fled from her in fear, but a small number of tainted souls swallowed their fear and approached her. She re-fused to answer to her once human name. She would only allow herself to be known as Nekhat, which was, she claim-ed, her true name.

She told this small number of souls that while in the wilderness she had become "awakened" to the tainted essence within herself. She revealed the story of the Dark and the Light, she told them of the Construct and its purpose, she told them the story of Leviathan. With her help this group of souls learned how to become aware of their own tainted essence, how to listen to it, and how to use it. They learned how to use their powers to fight the machines of the Construct, how to reach out and feel the Construct and know its movements, how to survive it.

As they grew in power they began to learn what they believed to be their true names, the verbal representation of the Darkness inside of them. Through long periods of meditation and guidance the small group became awakened. Nekhat forbid them to teach others, stating that since they were the only ones with the will to approach her, they were the only ones worthy of the power.

As time passed, even though they grew more and more powerful, they began to grow uncomfortable with Nekhat. She had begun making attempts to reach out to the Dark itself, and during the occasional skirmishes the group engaged in to hone their skills, Nekhat would reach out to the Dark with her powers and bring some of it back with her to use in the fighting. It was as if she was temporarily possessed by something from the Dark.

Eventually, many of the inhabitants of the Construct banded together to battle these demigods. During this pitched battle, Nekhat touched the Dark. This time, however, it consumed her, became her. Nekhat lashed out at anything or anyone within reach, friend and foe alike. During the resulting massacre, some of Nekhat's original followers managed to escape. Survivors of the massacre report Nekhat as having disappeared into the Construct.

She has not been seen since.

DIVERSE SIGNS

These most potent signs shall be so formed with thy left hand.

The first sign is that of Voor, and in nature it be the True symbol of the Old Ones. Make this whenever thou wouldst supplicate Those that ever wait beyond the Threshold.

The second sign is that of Kish, and it breaks down all barriers and opens the portals of the Ultimate Planes.

In the third place goes the Great Sign of Koth which Seals the Gates and guards the pathways.

The forth sign is that of the Elder Gods. It protects those who would evoke the powers by night, and banishes the forces of menace and antagonism.

The Elder Sign takes yet another form; the act of sacrifice and the Dying God. When so inscribed upon reality, it serves to hold back the power of The Great Old Ones for a time.

THE AWAKENING

In the time after Nekhat's disappearance, her disciples aught others, and many throughout the Construct became awakened to their taint. In time, that period became known as the Awakening, and the time of ignorant suffering before it became the Age of Strife. The Awakening was the beginning of a new age, one in which hope was born again, even if that hope did carry with it the taint of the Darkness. Since the majority cannot become one with their darkness, those who can, quickly become the rulers or the hunted.

THE REDEEMERS

Redeemers are biotech killing entities that unceasingly hunt the tainted souls. They are roughly humanoid, though twice the size of an average human. They are covered in alien looking segmented armor and carry a myriad of close combat weapons, some wickedly edged and others designed for bludgeoning.

While deadly in battle, they are relatively easy to spot and hear, as blinding beams of golden light constantly shine forth from the seams in their armor. A low droning sound issues from their unmoving heads, which are shapeless pillars of light. In the unlikely event that they are killed, the light dissipates and they fall in a heap of empty armor. Naturally, Redeemer weapons are highly valuable and a symbols of fear and status. Many think that they app-eared because the taint within the Construct had reached a higher level than ever before. More were surviving, so the Redeemers have come as a Construct security measure.

THE SCAR

This the area of the Construct that was damaged during Leviathan's assault. Though the Construct has somehow re-paired itself on the Darkside, there are still gaps in the Lightside security grid. For one reason or another, the Construct has been unable or unconcerned with the repair of those small breaches in its otherwise flawless system.

One of the more humane followers of Nekhat discovered it while wandering the Construct with a group of early Navigators, souls that have the innate gift to divine both direction and location within the Construct. It was discovered that if a tainted soul stood directly in the breach, there was a possibility of entering the Light. If a tainted soul leapt through the breach it would instantly be destroyed, but if a tainted soul were to step from the breach at the same instant a fresh soul was entering the Construct there was a way out.

If one passed through the breach, a tainted soul would find themselves enfleshed upon the earth with all of their powers intact. If death occurred, their taint was released into the Construct as before, but their human spirits were recycled into the Light. It was a sort of suicidal salvation. The Navigators and the Awakened One realized the vast and horrifying potential of this place. One could enter and return to the Light, but the temptation to use their powers to become gods would be too great for most tainted souls. So, after eliminating those of their number who were of less noble disposition, they decided to guard the Scar from further discovery or intrusion.

However, like all things, the years proved to be harsh and unforgiving. As the centuries passed by word spread of the Scar and its offer of reincarnation and godhood.

Many battles have been fought as multitudes of harrowed souls waged horrific wars for control of the area. It is thought that when the original Navigators and the Awakened One were killed that their human essence became a part of the Construct like everyone else. Yet after their deaths, the actual location of the Scar seems to shift from place to place within the Construct. Many believe that it was the dying will of the guardians that the Scar be a distant dream, the object of a spiritual quest and not a victory in arms.

Redeemers are said to frequent places in which the Scar will next appear, but few have dared approach. Those who have attempted it either die or succeed.

None have returned to tell the tale.

TO FASHION THE SAVAGE WEAPON

In the day and hour of Mars and when the Moon increases, make thou a blade of bronze with a hilt of fine ebony.

Upon one side of the blade thou shalt inscribe the dread name Hastur and his Yellow Sign.

On the day and hour of Saturn the moon decreasing, light thou a fire of Laurel boughs and whilst offering the blade to the flames, pronounce the five-fold conjuration thus:

I powerfully call upon you and stir the mighty spirits that dwell in the Great Abyss. In the dread and potent name of HASTUR come forth and give power unto this blade fashioned in accordance to ancient Lore.

Attend me! Give aid me! Give power unto my spell that this weapon which bears the runes of fire, receives such virtue that it shall strike fear into the hearts of all spirits that would disobey my commands. That it shall assist me to form all manner of Circles, Figures and Mystic Sigils necessary in the operations of Magickal Art.

In the Name of Great and Mighty Hastur and in the invincible sign of Voor (Make the sign of Voor)

Give power!
Give power!
Give power!

When the flames turn blue it shall be a sure sign that the spirits obey your demands whereupon thou shalt quench the blade in an afore prepared mixture of blood and brine.

Burn incense as an offering to the spirits thou hast called forth, then dismiss them to their abodes with these words:

(Make the Elder Sign)

I discharge thee; go forth from this place in peace and return the not until I call thee.

(Seal the portals with the sign of Koth).

Wrap the blade in a cloth of black silk and set it aside until thou wouldst make use of it, but mark well that no other shall lay his hand upon the blade lest its virtue be squandered by impure touch.

SPACE WITHIN THE CONSTRUCT

Most think the Construct is infinite. When one travels within the Construct, focus is usually on known areas or persons and the Construct slowly leads them there, making subtle changes along the way. Maps and landmarks are created and followed by using the death machines as reference points. The machines themselves do not move, whereas the paths that lead towards and away from them do.

Navigators use the death machines like stars to locate their position within the Construct. Those with awakened souls can use Construct Empathy powers to guide themselves without memorizing landmarks or using maps.

Recently, explorers have begun to venture deeper into the Construct than ever before. Most explorers are awakened souls because travel in unknown areas of the Construct is quite dangerous. Rumor has it that explorers are beginning to find proof that the Construct is, in actuality, finite.

BELIEFS AND RELIGION

Many see the construct as purgatory and feel that when they die, the good parts of them will go back into the light. Others see it as a testing ground. Those who are worthy when they die, join the Dark as their consciousness leaves with their taint.

 Most are completely atheistic and without hope for something better, thus they try to make their life in the Construct their main focus. Through the use of the taint power, Call the Void, some dark cults have arisen that focus on one or more of the outer darklings that have been discovered.

Some even rationalize an explanation of their own religion and that they are in hell, saying that the creators were god or Allah or Jehovah or Vishnu's angels, there are many ascetics amongst those who have spiritual ideals.

THE VOICE OF HASTUR

Hear the Voice of dread Hastur, hear the mournful sigh of the vortex, the mad rushing of the Ultimate Wind that Swirls darkly amongst the silent stars.

Hear the Him that howls serpent-fanged amid the bowels of nether earth; He whose ceaseless roaring ever fills the timeless skies.

His might tears the forest and crushes the city, but none shall know the hand that smites and the soul that destroys, for faceless and foul walks the Accursed One, His form to men unknown, hidden beneath the Pallid Mask of his King in Yellow.

Hear then His Voice in the dark hours, answer His call with thy own; bow and pray at His passing, but speak not His name aloud.

SOCIETY MACABRE

Most society is organized into small enclaves of varied sorts.

Some are organized around a religious or philosophical belief system, but most are heterogeneous groups held together by a need for survival and the ironclad rule of very powerful awakened souls. There are a scattered few bands of souls that live in equality, but as a general rule, society, if it can be called that, is a very loose, horrific, and violent state of affairs. Many groups are nothing more than roving bands of killers, because there isn't really much else to do in hell other than fight and survive in their eyes.

There is one group that is more the size of a tribe that resides in the supposed central area of the Construct, a place known to most as the Core. They are ruled by a very powerful monarch. At his side is a small order of theologians from as many points of view as he can manage to collect. It is one of the few societies in the Construct where it remains civil enough to warrant politics and positioning and power plays without open violence. Duels are common however, as a symbol of membership to the tribe, which is generally open to any, so long as they can pass the tests and submit to the unquestioned, and at times, fanatical lord. They are required to keep their heads shaven regardless of gender.

Almost every society in hell is feudalistic. Save for the scattered communist and council groups, democracy is almost nonexistent. It is about evenly split as to the ratio of groups that claim territory in one place in the Construct and those groups that just wander the Construct as nomads.

SKIN AND BONES

The unawakened wear clothing made from the skins of others. This skin turns black upon death, some believing this is the result of the stain left behind as the taint leaves the body. The awakened usually create their own clothing out of what appears to be darkness itself. Weapons and equipment come from the debris of dismantled death machines, though no one really had these things until Nekhat showed them how to destroy the machines. Even so, equipment, especially weapons, are uncommon and guarded as the most precious of possessions. Few have more than one weapon and one or two pieces of equipment, for without the need for food or sleep, there is not much need for basic items that sustain life.

CALL FORTH THE SHOGGOTH

For Yog-Sothoth is the Gate.

He knoweth from whence the Old Ones came forth in times past.

He knoweth from whence they shall came forth again with the return of the cycle.

When thou would call forth the children of Yog-Sothoth thou must wait until the Sun is in the Fifth House with Saturn in trine. Then enter within the stones and draw about thee the Circle of Evocation tracing the figurines with the Savage Weapon.

Circumambulate thrice widdershins and turning thy face to the South, intone the conjuration that opens the Gate.

THE CONJURATION

O Thou that dwells in the darkness of the Outer Void, come forth unto the Earth once more, I entreat thee.

O Thou who abides beyond the Spheres of Time, hear my supplication.

(Make the sign of Caput Draconis)
O Thou who art the Gate and the Way, come forth, come forth, Thy servant calls Thee.

(Make the Sign of Kish)

Come forth! Come forth! I speak the words, I Break Thy bonds, the seal is cast aside. Pass through
the Gate and enter the World as I make Thy mighty Sign!

(Make the Sign of the Voor)

Trace the pentagram of Fire and present the acts of violations and blood that causes the Great One to manifest before the Gate.

Then he will come unto thee and bring His children.
And when His hour be past, the curse of the Elder Lords shall be upon Him and draw Him forth beyond the Gate where He shall abide until He be summoned.

THE ABDJURATION OF GREAT CTHULHU

Ph'nglui mglw'nafh Cthulhu R'ltheh

Wgah'nagl fhtagn.

A supplication to great Cthulhu for those who would have power over his minions.

In the day and hour of the moon, with sun in Scorpio,

prepare thou a waxen tablet and inscribe thereon the seals of Cthulhu and Dagon; suffumigate with incense and set aside.

When the Walking Dead rise, thou must travel to some lonely place where high ground overlooks the ocean. Take up the tablet in thy right hand and make the sign of Kish with thy left. Recite the incantation thrice and when the final word of the third utterance dies in the air, cast thou the tablet into the waves saying:

In His House Dead Cthulhu waits dreaming. He shall rise and His kingdom shall cover the Earth.

He shall come unto you in sleep and show His sign with which you shall unlock the secrets of the deep.

THE INCANTATION

O Thou that lies dead, but ever dreaming, Hear Thy servant calling Thee. Hear me, O mighty Cthulhu!

Hear me Lord of Dreams!

In Thy tower at R'ltheh They have sealed thee, but Dagon shall break Thy accursed bonds, and Thy Kingdom shall rise once more. The Deep Ones know Thy secret Name, The Hydra knows Thy lair;

Give forth Thy sign that I may know Thy will upon the Earth. When death dies, Thy time shall be, and Thou shall sleep no more; Grant me the power to still the waves, that I may hear Thy Call.

At the third repeating of the incantation cast forth the Tablet into the waves saying:

In His House, Dead Cthulhu waits dreaming, there He Shall rise and His kingdom shall cover the Earth.

REALITY IS A PRISON

Awakened demigods and harrowed souls struggle to survive the Construct's death machines, hunted by almost unstoppable Redeemers and all the while battling with each other as the Construct attempts to grind them into nothing.

Some of us have escaped and returned to Earth to seek the Pallid Mask and to use the Book of the Black Earth. Some whisper that Nekhat is here, now, hunting those few of us who have sought to spread the truth of all things.

Take this knowledge, and seek your fate.

RECIPES

FRIED CHICKEN

Ain't no food better on this earth than fried chicken.

This is the staple of the slayer's culinary arsenal. You know how they say everything tastes like chicken? Yep, because for whatever reason chicken is good in just about any form, though, hell, yeah, fried is best. Fried chicken is the only food useful both for getting your hex on and for clearing away the tentacles in your head. Offense and defense, all in one little bird. Nobody knows why it's the chicken, maybe something dating back to the myth of the cockatrice, but that knowledge has been lost. Newbies some-times wonder if tofu could be used the same way, but as most of us with a little experience know, the dish don't work unless it's got animal product in it somewhere. It's the deep down magic of sacrifice, taking the life (or at least utilizing it) of another creature to further your purpose. Honestly it's the one advantage we have against the Mythos.

Animals die and we get our meat, milk, cheese, cooking oil, and eggs. In a lot of ways it might just be our reality struggling against theirs. Putting up blood against tentacle, so to speak. Regardless of the theories, meat does the trick and no meat does it like chicken, especially fried. So next time you see a chicken, you thank that poor bastard before you fry him up.

1 (4 pound) chicken, cut into pieces
1 cup buttermilk
2 cups all-purpose flour (throw some cornmeal
in there for grit)
1 tsp paprika
salt and pepper to taste
2 quarts vegetable oil for frying

Take your cut up chicken pieces, skin 'em if you prefer, but most of us old hands leave the skin on, just tastes better that way. Put the flour in a large plastic bag (let the amount of chicken you are cooking dictate the amount of flour you use). Season the flour with paprika, salt and pepper to taste. If you're in the mood for something with a bit more kick throw on some cajun seasoning or just plain old cayenne pepper.

Dip chicken pieces in buttermilk then, a few at a time, put them in the bag with the flour, seal the bag and shake to coat well. Place the coated chicken on a cookie sheet or tray, and cover with a clean dish towel or waxed paper. The flour needs to be more like a paste, so let it sit for a bit. This is a fine opportunity to take another swig of your hooch.

Fill a large skillet (cast iron is best because iron has a natural tendency to break up and dissipate magical energy, so you're infusing your meal with more of that cleansing mojo) about 1/3 to 1/2 full with vegetable oil. Heat until it's piping hot. Put in as many chicken pieces as the skillet can hold. Brown the chicken in hot oil on both sides. When browned, reduce heat and cover skillet. Let it cook for 30 minutes (the chicken will be cooked through, but not too crispy). Remove cover, raise heat again and continue to fry until crispy.

Drain the fried chicken on paper towels. Depending on how much chicken you have, you may have to fry in a few shifts, but that's where it's good to have a partner or a whole crew with you, so one can cook while the others eat and drink, that way nobody loses their mind waiting. Keep the finished chicken in a slightly warm oven while preparing the rest, though we all know you're likely to wolf all of it down to stave off the crazy or get yourself hexed up, so leftovers don't happen too much.

CHEESEBURGER MEATLOAF

I like meatloaf, cheeseburgers and kicking tentacled ass (yikes, that's a mental image). When I can put all three together, I'm one happy camper. This is a cleansing recipe, total comfort food for the weary slayer hoping to stave off inevitable insanity for a little while longer. It has all the good stuff I like about cheeseburgers without all those pesky healthy bits like lettuce, served up meatloaf style. This and a cold one will fix you up right as rain.

2 pounds ground beef
3/4 cup bread crumbs
1/2 cup minced onion
2 eggs, beaten
1 1/2 tsps ground black pepper
1 1/2 tsps salt

4 cups shredded Cheddar cheese
or jack cheese if you like it spicy)

Preheat oven to 350 degrees F (175 degrees C). While you're waiting go ahead and munch about a cup of that shredded cheese and wash it down with a brew, you've earned it.
In a large bowl, mix up the beef, bread crumbs, onion, eggs, salt and pepper, and whip the heck out of it. Pat out meat mixture into a 14x18 inch rectangle on a piece of wax paper. Spread cheese over the meat, leaving a 3/4 inch border around the edges. Roll it up like a homemade cigarette to enclose the filling and form a pinwheel loaf. Press beef in on both ends to enclose the cheese. Place in a 10x15 inch baking dish.

Bake in the preheated oven 1 hour, or until internal temperature reaches 165 degrees F (75 degrees C). Then pull it out, slice and serve right away, because after your people smell this they won't want to wait a second longer.

PORK CHOPS

Pigs are smart animals, way smarter than anybody gives 'em credit for. Modern pigs are the domesticated descendants of the wild boar, or as we call 'em around here 'razorbacks'. What most folks don't know is that the Pig God was one of the ancient enemies of the Old Ones.

Back in those primordial days, when the old powers still had purchase on this plane, there were creatures wandering the wilderness that still bore the mark of their dark progenitors.

What I'm gettin' at here is that there were a bunch of creatures that weren't much more than a heap of tentacles and teeth. They didn't worship nothing per se, but they sure were some killing machines, and as the slave beasts of the old ones, every kill was a sacrifice. Well, hear tell is, the Pig God was one of the star players in the resistance of natural beasts against these walking nightmares. They say that the children of the Pig God still have a spark of the badassery of their ancestor, and if you've ever had occasion to eat yourself some pig flesh you know what I mean. The closer to the wilderness you can get, the better, be-cause the more like their divine ancestor the pig you're eating has been able to live, the more mojo they've got stored up inside 'em. There's a big argument here for humane treatment of these once noble creatures, beyond the fact that it's just plain ole the right thing to do.

The more wilderness they've got in their blood, the more powerful. You maximize that power by taking 'em down yourself.

Pig hunting is an easy way to die.

Those sumbitches are vicious if you catch 'em on the wrong morning, but there's no sweeter meat than what you take with your own hands and there's no mojo more heavy duty than in game you killed in the wild.

Through the years, some of the more hardcore of my buddies have taken to hunting wild boar with nothing but their bowie knives. I swear by the light of the moon that knife-killed wild boar chops will soak up darkness that would otherwise land you in the nuthouse. Living off the land like that is one of the only reasons Papa Proctor is still able to speak in complete sentences. Hell, he keeps the skulls and says they whisper things to him, give him advice, tell him of warnings, and keep him safe when he's sleeping. Now, I don't know about all that for sure, he's a strange one indeed, but if that's how he does it then so be it.

Here follows how I like to cook up my chops, whether they're wild like they oughta be, or store bought in a pinch. I grill 'em or roast 'em over an open fire, and that's it. No oil frying, no baking, no glazing, no nothing. If you're wondering why I ain't included any recipe for pork chops, ham hocks, bacon or any other kind of pig flesh, it's because throwing the meat on a hot cooking surface is all you need to do.

Cooking pork with anything other than heat and a pinch of salt is a sinister bit of disinformation that got circulated by one cult or another, starting back in the bronze age or maybe even before. That's another one of those little mysteries of the Mythos. If you put anything on pig flesh other than a pinch of salt, you'll dissipate any of the mojo that's clinging to it. No matter how much ham or bacon you put down your gullet, you won't cleanse yourself of a damn thing. Believe me, it's a dirty shame, because there are so many tasty ways to eat yourself some pig, but all of it is a lie that's been propagated to rob the Pig God's children of their power, to keep them from coming to the aide of us humans. Any other kind of meat you can cook up however you want, but because the pigs specifically stood in the way of the shoggoths of the age, they've been cursed and targeted and lied about.

I know it's a tough one, buddy, I've been there, but you have to just cook your meat and eat it without putting a dress on it.

Thankfully, our porcine friends are mighty tasty on their own.

BEEF POT ROAST

I whip this up the way my mama used to make it, and her mama, and as far back as the Bartlett line goes, or at least that's what grandma said.

Now of the Bartlett clan, it's just me in my generation that's a slayer. My own son just wasn't the sort of kid who had the shine to him; never had that deep restlessness that makes you look harder at the world to see what's really there. He was a good boy, and though he never grew up to be a man, good or otherwise, I like to imagine that he had himself a crop of youngsters I could bounce on my knee someday when I was too old or useless to do much else.

I've never had any more family after my first. Officially, on account of me being a wanted man in most states of this great nation. I've never been able to keep a woman happy, even after having a youngun or two, but I've look-ed in on all of them time and again. No, the rest of my family was blessed with as normal a life as they come, and for that I'm plenty thankful.

Far as my kin knows, I killed me a few men in Memphis and been on the run ever since. By now they probably think I'm dead. I did set my eye on two of my sister's grandkids though. She married a drifter, one of those tall, dark, and handsome fellas who has more charm than good in him. Left her with two boys and a broken heart, but she did her best, and in DeValls Bluff your best is sometimes just putting food on the table and a roof over the head.

Around town they're known as the Bartlett Brothers, a pair of tubby rednecks who could out-drink, out-smoke, and out-fight anybody they were likely to meet. There was a loup garou problem in town, and those boys were there to get into the thick of it. They didn't make it out alive, but I reckon they earned a place in this here book.

When a man is faced with the terrible truth that there are monsters and dark magic at work in the world, he can curl up and die or he can stand up and fight, even if he's still likely to die.

Me and Danny Jenkins were the only two people at their funeral, which was closed casket, like every slayer I've ever known to die. Danny was the one who told me how things went down, starting off with a bullshit story about a wild dog pack, then of course, after sharing a bottle of whiskey for the dead and me showing him my trunk full of weapons and witchcraft, he told me the truth about those shape shifting sons of bitches.

My sister served up this pot roast at their wake later that night, and after all the shit he'd been through I made sure Danny when back for seconds. He's back in rehab for a meth addict-ion, and my sister moved out of town, but every time I serve up this dish I think about my mama, my sister, the departed Bartlett Brothers, and Danny.

It tastes like home.

1 (5 pound) bone-in beef pot roast
salt and pepper to taste

1 tblsp all purpose flour, or more as needed
2 tblsps vegetable oil
8 ozs. Sliced mushrooms
1 medium onion, chopped
2 cloves garlic, minced
1 tblsp butter
1/2 tblsps all purpose flour
1 tblsp tomato paste
2 1/2 cups chicken broth
3 medium carrots, cut into chunks
2 stalks celery, cut into chunks
1 sprig fresh rosemary
2 sprigs fresh thyme

Generously season both sides of roast with salt and pepper. Sprinkle flour over the top until well coated, and pat it into the meat. Shake off any excess. Heat vegetable oil in a large skillet over medium-high heat until hot. Sear the roast on both sides for 5-6 minutes each, until well browned. Remove from the skillet and set aside.

Reduce the heat to medium and stir in mushrooms and butter; cook for 3-4 minutes. Stir in onion; cook for 5 minutes, until onions are translucent and begin to brown. Add garlic, stir for about a minute. Stir in 1 1/2 tablespoons flour; cook and stir for about 1 minute. Add tomato paste, and cook for another minute. Slowly add chicken stock, stir to combine, and return to a simmer. Remove skillet from the heat. Place carrots and celery in the slow cooker. Place roast over the vegetables and pour in any accumulated juices. Add rosemary and thyme. Pour onion and mushroom mixture over the top of the roast. Cover slow cooker, turn to high and cook the roast for 5-6 hours, until the meat is fork tender.

Skim off any fat from the surface and remove the bones. Season with salt and pepper to taste. The fat and bones can be re-purposed as candles, as they'll still be charged with some of the mojo of the cooking and the meal. If you burn these, they can dispel some of the ambient darkness in any room. While they won't do a full cleanse, they can at least clear out the cobwebs if you find yourself in a situation where you need a little boost, but don't have the time or tools to whip up a meal.

BUTTERMILK BEER PANCAKES

If you don't like pancakes you're either a terrorist or a shoggoth and even some of them have learned about the tasty joy of a hot pancake slathered in real butter and something sweet.

Personally, I like molasses, but I'm an old man with old ways, so I'm sure you young bucks can find yourself some organic maple syrup or some kinda raw honey. I have lost count of how many times I've opted to have breakfast in the middle of the night, especially since in the middle of the night is typically when all hell breaks loose.

Now you know as well as I do, that after a brawl with the bad guys you probably aren't looking fit for public consumption, smelling and looking like you've just fought and killed a squid the size of a man, since possibly, you have. As such, carrying a bag or plastic container of pancakes can get you through those initial crazy shakes and buy you some time to get to a kitchen or a shower, then a diner.

Now lots of folks have their own way of making pancakes, but I like to pour a healthy measure of beer in mine. I do this for two reasons, the first being that's how my daddy made 'em, the second is for that little bump to your juice. Not all slayers are hexers, but as I am, them's the terms I tend to think in. If I'm in dire straits enough to need emergency food to hold off the crazy shakes, then I could probably do with a little extra juice in case I'm only one hex away from getting perished. These pancakes won't hold much of a charge, but they'll hold just enough for that parting shot, if you need it. Since we've already talked the factory farming problem, if you do have to hit a diner, try to go to the local shop and avoid the chains. The local spot is more likely to have tastier food, poss-ibly some of it farmed locally, and those chain spots in addition to crappy food are more highly trafficked.

    Pancakes are my favorite and recommended emergency food, second only to fried chicken, and sometimes damn fine when paired with some fried chicken. Pancakes are essentially a dessert that has been culturally accepted as a standard breakfast item and tasty com-fort food. You can whip up a batch of these, enjoy 'em while they're hot, and stash the rest for backup. They keep for several days, even unrefrigerated, so are great for long road trips, which is an advantage they have over anything with meat. They won't cleanse you the way a full meal will, but again, these are a great first course in a hearty breakfast or as a grab and go when you have to move fast.

1 cup flour
1 tsp salt
1 tsp baking soda
1 egg
3/4 cup buttermilk
3/4 cup beer
2 tblsps butter, melted

Preheat and lightly grease a large skillet or electric griddle. Mix the flour, salt, and baking soda together in a bowl. Add the egg, buttermilk, beer, and butter, then whip the heck out of it. The batter should look puffy and smooth. As the beer tends to bubble, you'll have to really put some elbow into it.

Drop 1/3 cup of the batter onto the cooking surface, spreading lightly with the bottom of the cup. If you can make a Mickey Mouse shape or maybe a dinosaur like when you were a kid, cheesy as it sounds, you won't be able to help but crack a smile. That'll do you some good. Cook until lightly-browned on each side, 1 to 2 minutes per side depending on heat.

RONNIE'S BADASS GOAT CHILI

In addition to having the gift of tinkering and gunsmithing, my friend, Ronnie Fix, is one hell of a chili cook. How good? Well, let's put it this way, if he wasn't deep in hiding from the law, there wouldn't be a chili cook-off that he couldn't win. I keep a bottle of antacid in the glove box any time I know I'm gonna be running with Fix, because I know that I'll end up wolfing down more than I need and that's the price of over-indulgence.

To look at Ronnie you'd never think he was the sort of fellow who would consider good red wine to be a central ingredient in his chili, though like other dishes that are a mix of cleansing and a touch of mojo, it hits the spot when you need it most.

1 pound chopped Goat chunks
salt and pepper to taste
3 cans dark red kidney beans
3 cans stewed tomatoes
2 stalks celery, chopped
1 red bell pepper, chopped
1/4 cup red wine vinegar
2 tblsps chili powder
1 tsp ground cumin
1 tsp dried parsley
1 tsp dried basil
1 dash Worcestershire sauce
1 cup good red wine

In a large skillet over medium-high heat, cook the goat chunks until evenly browned. As with other foods the closer to the animal you can be, the more power you'll be able to employ in the dish. Ronnie keeps his own goats, and though goats aren't as fine tasting as sheep or cows, they're easier to raise when you're living off the grid. Besides, it makes his chili taste rather unique, so my advice is to do whatever you gotta do and spend the extra cash on good goat meat.

Drain off the grease and season to taste with salt and pepper. In a slow cooker, combine the cooked meat, kidney beans, tomatoes, celery, red bell pepper, and red wine vinegar. Season with chili powder, cumin, parsley, basil and Worcestershire sauce. Stir to distribute ingredients evenly. Cook on High for 6 hours, or on Low for 8 hours. Pour in the wine during the last 2 hours.

Some folks might look askance at an entire cup of wine, much less a fine, high end wine, but Ronnie swears by it, as does anyone whose tasted it. The chili will be a bit more soupy than most of what you've encountered, but that extra bit of liquid and flavor goes a long way.

Being a sorcerer and all, I also happen to think that Ronnie's insistence that you use only high end wine makes it a sort of sacrifice, especially since most slayers are cash strapped most of the time. That little touch of sacrifice will boost the potency of the food's magic.

BRISKET AND POTATO SOUP

As a kid, my favorite food in the winter was my momma's brisket and potato soup. It put a warmth in your belly with its broth and the rest of it stuck to your ribs in the best of ways.

Something my folks instilled in me early on was family supper in the winters. Since the crops were gone and game was scarce, there wasn't much else to do. Everybody would sit around the table and suck down a bowl or two of her soup, soak up what was left with some dinner rolls or flatbread, then we'd all retire to the porch to play music. I wish I could say we were good at it, but honestly there weren't a musical bone in any of our bodies. It ended up mostly being voices wailing and my daddy pitifully plucking on an old acoustic guitar that was as out of tune as the rest of us, but we had fun, and it's only now, in my old age, I see that was the whole point.

This here recipe is meant to bring you back to that old feeling, like the soup your momma used to make, the kind that keeps you smiling and keeps you warm.

1 1/2 pounds potatoes, peeled and diced
1 medium onion, diced
1 medium carrot, diced
1 rib celery, diced
8 ounces smoked brisket, shredded
3 cloves garlic, sliced
3 tblsps butter
1/4 cup flour
4 cups chicken broth
2 cups water
1/2 cup heavy cream
salt and pepper to taste
cayenne pepper (optional)
chopped fresh chives for garnish (optional)

Melt butter in a stockpot over medium heat until golden brown. Stir in carrot, celery, onion, brisket, and garlic; cook and stir for 5-6 minutes, until the vegetables soften and the onions are pretty darn clear. Stir in flour; cook for about 3 minutes.

Stir in chicken broth, 1 cup at a time. I know that takes a minute, but that's a perfect opportunity to have yourself a cold one while you take your time with this. Again, this is comfort food, so even cooking it should be an act of cleansing. You're pouring in love and mojo as you make it, never forget that.

Add water and stir to combine. Turn the heat to high and bring to a simmer. Simmer on medium-low for 15 minutes, stirring occasionally. Taste the soup for salt and add more if necessary. Stir in potatoes; cook for 15 minutes, until potatoes are tender. Some folks will tell you to skim the fat, well by now you should know that you need that fat to stay in, that's all part of the dish, plus it makes everything taste better.

With a potato masher, mash the soup a few times, leaving plenty of whole chunks of potato. Season with salt and pepper to taste, add cayenne if desired, and add cream. Stir to combine and heat through. Garnish with fresh chives.

There's a barbeque joint in DeValls Bluff called Craig's BBQ. Craig was an old conjure man who got himself drafted in WWII and after surviving the Battle of the Bulge, decided he'd had enough of fighting and war. He settled down in DeValls Bluff and started smoking meats and mixing up his special sauce out of his home kitchen and the rest is history. He put his magic into his meats and sauces and no matter how hard the supernatural shitstorms came down on that godforsaken town he refused to get involved.

It woulda pissed me off if his cooking wasn't so ding dang good.

He uses a Memphis style rub on the meat, and the sauce has some kind of mustard thing going on. He died about ten years ago, the only magic slinger I've ever heard of to pass gracefully in his sleep. Now his kin run the shop and they cook the way he cooked. Even though their work doesn't have the mojo that Craig's did, it still tastes damn good. If you ever find yourself in DeValls Bluff working a case, or just passing through, do yourself a favor and pick up a few sandwiches for the road and a few pounds of their smoked brisket.

CHICKEN POT PIE

If there was ever a meal that I'd be fine being my last one, I'd want it to be chicken pot pie. I'll admit that it's personal preference, but hear me out on this one. Most folks in this country have experienced hard times at some point in their life, and when you're down to your last dollar there's nothing you can buy that'll keep you going the way chicken pot pie will. Even those shitty frozen pot pies go down like a slice of heaven, because if you're eating one you've already hit rock bottom and nothing will taste better.

As we've discussed, the more processed a food the less mojo its gonna be able to give you, so of course you've gotta keep that in mind.

When I'm not living on the dodge and trying to eat off of my last dollar, I bake one of the better chicken pot pies in the south and I don't mind saying so. The thing about chicken pot pies is, they combine several kinds of cooking and all that prep work serves to infuse the food even more. They have the flashy and fast mojo of a quick boil or a pan fry (like a shrimp boil or fried catfish), but that's combined with the slow and deep mojo of a long baking.

While a frozen pot pie will keep you alive, the homemade pie is one of the most powerful cleansing foods out there, especially if I'm making it. My pot pies are more powerful than most folks because I love pot pies, they're my favorite dish to cook, and to eat, so that love I've got for the food boosts its already heavy duty intrinsic energetic properties.

When the cook loves you, that has power, more if the cook loves to cook, even more if the cook loves you and what they're cooking. It's called exponential energetic compounding, or at least that's what Papa Proctor used to call it. Then again, in the last years I was around him, he'd be saying that while boiling up what he claimed was rabbit and carrot stew.

(I'd be a liar though, if I didn't say that I thought I saw some severed rat-tails hiding in this trash pile).

1 pound skinless, boneless chicken breast halves - cubed
1 cup sliced carrots
1 cup frozen green peas
1/2 cup sliced celery
1/3 cup butter
1/3 cup chopped onion
1/3 cup all purpose flour
1/2 tsp salt
1/4 tsp black pepper
1/4 tsp celery seed
1 3/4 cups chicken broth
2/3 cup milk
2 (9 inch) unbaked pie crusts

Don't get me wrong, it's okay to buy pre-made pie crusts, but if you want to really to yourself a favor, go ahead and get a few crusts whipped up and frozen prior to any cooking you might do. Preheat oven to 425 degrees F (220 degrees C.) I recommend you double the recipe and make two. If you're doing things right, you'll have at least one friend who ain't dead, disappeared, or in an asylum that you might want to break bread with.

In a saucepan, combine that chicken, carrots, peas, and celery. Add water to cover and boil for 15 minutes. That 15 minutes could easily be used to suck down a cold one, or maybe two, if you're needing some extra juice while you wait.

Always, and I mean ALWAYS have a few beers handy, even if it's just cans of the cheap shit, because some of this good cooking can take a bit to prep, cook, and serve, especially if it's just you in the kitchen. If there's some heavy darkness putting the squeeze on you, more often than not, you can fortify yourself with a few brews while you wait for the cleansing food. I've known at least two fellas who ended up eating their guns because they got overwhelmed before they could finish the cook.

That can happen if you aren't careful.

Remove from heat, drain and set aside. In the saucepan, over medium heat, cook onions in butter until soft and translucent. Stir in flour, salt, pepper, and celery seed. Slowly stir in chicken broth and milk. Simmer over medium-low heat until thick. Remove from heat and set aside. Place the chicken mixture in bottom pie crust. Pour hot liquid mixture over. Cover with top crust, seal edges, and cut away excess dough. Make several small slits in the top to allow steam to escape. Bake in the preheated oven for 30 to 35 minutes, or until pastry is golden brown and filling is bubbly. Cool for 10 minutes before serving.

LASAGNA

This here is another one of those dishes that really takes some dedication and patience to pull off, which I know can be real hard if you've already got the crazy shakes. My suggestion is to keep this recipe in your back pocket as something to use when you aren't going solo. Not only is it the sort of dish that's best served in large portions to a group of people, you'll have some other folks to back you up in the kitchen on this one. Plenty of other meals you can make if you're own, but this one is sure to be a crowd pleaser if you are working with a group. If there's more than one slayer sitting down to do some clean-sing damage to a heaping plate of food, then I'm going to assume that you've just had to deal with the kind of cultist-shoggoth-elder-god-shitstorm that deserves a giant lasagna.

Be sure to throw a few drinks at folks while they're waiting. Even serving this up as leftovers it's pretty good. That's one of the cool powers of this particular dish, for whatever reason (I'm guessing all the layered pasta makes a symbolic net for the energy) lasagna doesn't lose as much mojo on the second go around, which most food does.

1 pound sweet Italian Sausage
2 cloves garlic, crushed
3/4 pound lean ground beef
1/2 cup minced onion
1 (28 oz) can crushed tomatoes
2 (6 oz) cans tomato paste

2 (6.5 oz) cans canned tomato sauce
1/2 cup water
2 tblsps white sugar
1 1/2 tsps dried basil leaves
1/2 teaspoon fennel seeds
1 tsp Italian seasoning
1 tblsp salt
1/4 tsp ground black pepper
4 tblsps chopped fresh parsley
12 lasagna noodles
16 ozs. ricotta cheese
1 egg
1/2 teaspoon salt
3/4 pound mozzarella cheese, sliced
3/4 cup grated Parmesan cheese

In a Dutch oven (if possible, I mean you could panfry, but the campfire is another important part of the group cleansing, as it allows folks to drink, chat, smoke, or whatever while they wait), cook sausage, ground beef, onion, and garlic over medium heat until well browned. Stir in crushed tomatoes, tomato paste, tomato sauce, and water. Season with sugar, basil, fennel seeds, Italian seasoning, 1 tablespoon salt, pepper, and 2 tablespoons parsley. Simmer, covered, for about 1 1/2 hours, stirring occasionally. Bring a large pot of lightly salted water to a boil. Cook lasagna noodles in boiling water for 8 to 10 minutes. Drain noodles, and rinse with cold water. In a mixing bowl, combine ricotta cheese with egg, remaining parsley, and 1/2 teaspoon salt.

Preheat oven to 375 degrees F (190 degrees C).To assemble, spread 1 1/2 cups of meat sauce in the bottom of a 9x13 inch baking dish. Arrange 6 noodles lengthwise over meat sauce. Spread with one half of the ricotta cheese mixture. Top with a third of mozzarella cheese slices. Spoon 1 1/2 cups meat sauce over mozzarella, and sprinkle with 1/4 cup Parmesan cheese. Repeat layers, and top with remaining mozzarella and Parmesan cheese. Other folks will tell you to cover it with foil, but I don't bother, as I like the taste of all the crispy bits at the top when you leave it uncovered. Bake in preheated oven for 25 minutes. Remove foil, and bake an additional 25 minutes. Cool for 15 minutes before serving.

CHOCOLATE CHIP COOKIES

There are two kinds of people in this world. Those who admit to eating raw cookie dough and those who lie about it, because we've all done it. I'm sure you're getting tired of hearing it, but you guessed it, the less industrialized and more natural your eggs and other ingredients the better the dough and the final cookies will be in the taste, health, and mojo packing departments.

These work a bit like pancakes, in that they're good road food for that quick cleanse to keep your mind and spirit held together by at least a thread or two while you burn rubber towards a kitchen and a real meal. Here's a little trade secret for you, the shoggoths love 'em. Yessir, those slavering nightmares can't pass up a good chocolate chip cookie. It's kind of like throwing a juicy steak at a pissed off guard dog, they're confused because they want to sink their teeth into the steak just as much as they want to sink 'em into you. That moment of hesitation is your opportunity for fight or flight.

I don't rightly know what it is about chocolate chip cookies that seems to do it, and I can't say it has worked every time, but it works often enough that I do my best to keep a few handy. Maybe it's the sugar and general confectionary goodness, which makes a kind of sense I guess, as lots of the old gods like sweets as part of their ritual feasts and sacrifices. Maybe that holds true for servants and monsters of the Elder Gods as well. Just remember, if you chuck one and it does work, you've got maybe a second or two before the beast is back at you, so make your play fast. I'm still breathing because I've been lucky enough to fight when I can win and flee when I couldn't, and Lord knows I've been gambling as to which is which. Sometimes that extra second means one or two more clouds of buckshot you can send its way, or the difference between making it to your vehicle or getting grabbed just shy of escape.

4 1/2 cups all purpose flour
2 tsps baking soda
2 cups butter, softened
1 1/2 cups packed brown sugar

1 tblsp of ground coffee
4 eggs
2 tsps vanilla extract
4 cups semi sweet chocolate chips

Preheat oven to 350 degrees F (175 degrees C). Sift together, the flour and baking soda, set aside. You'll notice, of course, that I have a bit less sugar in my recipe than most folks, and instead of some of that sugar I put in a bit of ground coffee. First off, I like the hint of coffee in my cookies and after you try it you'll agree, it's something special. Second, I think you can mask all the rest of the ingredients with too much sugar, and because I like to taste as much as I can, the full range of the cookie as it were, I put in less sugar. Just be-cause it's a confection doesn't mean it is supposed to only have one flavor. That kind of thinking is how the food industry has pulled the wool over your eyes, or your taste-buds as it were. Expect more out of your food, and put in the work when it comes to prep and cook, and the food will meet you half-way, both in taste and in empowerment.

In a large bowl, cream together, the butter, brown sugar, and ground coffee. Stir in the eggs and vanilla. Blend in the flour mixture. Finally, stir in the chocolate chips. Drop cookies by round-ed spoonfuls onto ungreased cookie sheets, you should probably go ahead and plan on making a baker's dozen, be-cause I guarantee you'll eat one raw by the time you get the rest into the oven. Bake for 10 to 12 minutes in the preheated oven. Edges should be golden brown.

APPLE PIE

Remember back when I said I wasn't going to talk about food that wasn't meant for cleansing and that's why there ain't no Cajun cooking in this book? Well, I wasn't entirely honest with you and for that I apologize.

Apple Pie is one of the few foods that is both an empowerment and has a specific sort of hex tied to it, and it's so insidiously prevalent in American culture that I had to talk about it here. Plus, it's useful as hell if you can bring enough rampage to the table to make good on the hex. I'm sure you've seen a cartoon or two in which Mickey Mouse or Bugs Bunny or What's-his-name is walking along minding his own business when the gently waft-ing scent of a fresh-baked apple pie wafts up his nose. Then the character is lifted off his or her feet and pulled through the air to the inevitable windowsill upon which rests a delicious looking apple pie. Inevitably, that's when the antics ensue. Well, pilgrim, those cartoons are based in truth, only it's a lot darker and bloodier than you'd ever have thought.

Shoggoths are suckers for sweets, and like the trick with the cookies, they usually can't resist a tasty thing that's been cooked with power. The combination of sweetness with the mojo makes it damn near impossible for them to avoid. Folks through the years have wondered why it doesn't work with other sweets, and why it does work with apple pie.
General bush wisdom is that there's a connection between the fruits of the tree of life and the pie. To me it makes all the sense in the world. On

the one hand, you have Eve take the fruit and she is infused with the know-ledge of the tree. She then passes it to Adam, and human history starts to unfold from there.

 Sure, I know it's probably just a story, but it has some heavy duty truth to it. The serpent is a symbol of wisdom and cunning in just about every culture, and the Tree of Life is also present in most world cultures.

I'm not sure if it's because of Walt Disney or Moses or both that the apple became the symbolic fruit, but it did and that's what matters. You bake a badass apple pie and it not only has all the mojo and tastiness of a home-made pie, but it's made with, at least symbolically, which means energetic-ally, the fruit of the tree of life. If you look at apple pie in that way, then it makes all the sense in the world that when a shoggoth catches the scent of a fresh baked apple pie they'll come for it, which makes the apple pie a useful way to lure in a shoggoth.

You heard me. Setting out a fresh apple pie when you're inside a known cult zone is a somewhat reliable way of flushing out any shoggoths that the cult might have summoned, or, if you're in Louisiana and parts of Arkansas you could draw out wyld shoggoths that are already manifested in the swamps and caves.

I couldn't tell you what the scent range is, as it all depends on the sensory capacities of the shoggoths in question, and I know it's crazy talking about the effective tactical range of an apple pie, but these are strange days my friend. When they come looking for the pie you had better be ready with some serious hexing and firepower, because they are going to be all riled up and hungry. Sure, they'll go for the pie first, but that'll only give you a few seconds before they turn their attention to you, and don't forget that unless it's a wyld shoggoth who serves no master, the sorcerer or cult that controls the shoggoth won't be far behind their minion.

It goes without saying that you shouldn't attempt this on your own, regardless of whatever tall tales you might have heard about Papa Proctor. Better to be rolling several slayers deep before even bothering thinking of this as a course of action. That being said, it sure beats fishing for clues if you're on a case and have no leads.

1 recipe pastry for a 9" double
Crust pie
1/2 cup unsalted butter
3 tblsps all purpose flour
1/4 cup water
1/2 cup white sugar
1/2 cup packed brown sugar
8 Granny Smith apples, peeled, cored and sliced

Preheat oven to 425 degrees F (220 degrees C). Melt the butter in a saucepan. Stir in flour to form a paste. Add water, white sugar and brown sugar, and bring to a boil. Reduce temperature and let simmer. Place the bottom crust in your pan. Fill with apples, mounded slightly. Cover with a lattice work crust. Gently pour the sugar and butter liquid over the crust. Pour slowly so that it does not run off. Bake 15 minutes in the preheated oven. Reduce the temperature to 350 degrees F (175 degrees C). Continue baking for 35 to 45 minutes, until apples are soft.

Remove from oven and set on open air windowsill or acceptable platform. I've only done this twice in my life, and both times we set up a box fan to carry the scent onto the wind, and though I'm not sure where in those shitburg little towns the shoggoths were holed up, but not more than twenty minutes later (both times) they came barreling into range. Stock up on ammo and booze for the fight, and have a robust meal prepped and ready to cook for the aftermath, preferably in a kitchen different than the one you made the apple pie in, because believe me, that one is going to get wrecked.

CHICKEN AND DUMPLIN'S

There aren't very many slayers left these days, not that our numbers have ever been all that large, so some of the old ways are dying along with us geezers when we go. Cynicism and disinformation seems to me, to be enemies to humanity that are just as powerful as a frenzied shoggoth or a well-funded and motivated cult. The enemy doesn't have to kill us so much as it just has to wait. Then again, that's how it's always been, with us outnumbered and outgunned, but somehow we keep the hammer from dropping.

A friend of mine, who went on to be an FBI field agent before disappearing somewhere up in Washington state, told me "There is no future, so get used to the taste of ashes." It's a zero sum game, but we have to play it, or else there would be nothing but the darkness. That being said, just because we've been dealt a shitty hand by the universe, doesn't mean we can't live it up while we're here. That same FBI agent also had this to say "Give yourself a present every day". Therein lies the wisdom, and in no better dish is it expressed than in a good mess of chicken and dumplins.

As you'll see below, it takes just shy of seven hours to cook, and that ain't including the prep time. This is a dish that the young bucks don't ever seem to work with, or just plain don't have the patience for, but there's a subtle power to it that should be noted. The slayer who preps the food and throws it in the slow cooker is telling the universe, by his or her actions, that there is an intention to survive the coming ordeal. You set this dish up, go do your business, and come back in seven hours for a tasty meal. This ain't something you cook when you get back, no sir, you set this up expecting to come back, and that has big mojo brother.

4 skinless, boneless chicken breast halves
2 tblsps butter
2 (10.75 oz) cans condensed cream of chicken soup
1 onion, finely diced
2 (10 oz) packages refrigerated biscuit dough, torn into pieces

Place the chicken, butter, soup, and onion in a slow cooker, and fill with enough water to cover. Put the lid on the cooker, and cook for 5 to 6 hours on High. About 30 minutes before serving, place the torn biscuit dough in the slow cooker. Cook until the dough is no longer raw in the center. Nothing, and I mean nothing, tastes better than a fine meal from a slow cooker that you set up before diving into the darkness.

Give yourself a present every day.

SLOPPY JOES

I don't know about you, but I've got nothing but good memories about Sloppy Joes. For whatever reason, that dish was a constant fixture in my teenage years. We'd scrape together enough cash for beer, beef, buns, and a few gallons of gas for Bobby Yeager's boat. It wasn't the biggest or the best, but that barge would hold at least ten people comfortably, fifteen if at least five of them folks was ladies, if you know what I mean.

We'd haul ourselves out to the White River, just outside of Clarendon, Arkansas, and have ourselves a little party on the water. Seems like every Saturday that's where we'd be. It seemed important to make that happen. The faces would change, as folks sometimes had to work, and others disappeared entirely, leaving for Vietnam, prison, or fates unknown. Those were heady, even chaotic, times.

Apparently, I'm not the only geezer from the South who had those kinds of memories. Even some of those young bucks out there who came up in the 80's and 90's thought likewise. There's a recklessness to Sloppy Joes, a kind of maniac party mojo that hides in plain sight, somewhere in between the bun and the sauce. It's like sweet chili served up as a sandwich, which means as long as you've got a hot pot of the good stuff and a case of cold ones then you can start up a party anywhere.

Sloppy Joes really are meant to be enjoyed in large groups. They are unique in that you can still get the mojo even if you're with a group that's clueless about the Mythos. Yessir, that is one of the unique powers of the 'Joe', it can cleanse you just by sharing it with others. Of course good ingredients help, but the real trick with this dish is fellowship, because at the end of the day what the hell else are we fighting for but our fellow man and woman?

1 pound lean ground beef
1/4 cup chopped onion
1/4 cup chopped green bell pepper (or a jalapeno if you're feeling like a badass)
1/2 tsp garlic powder
1 tsp prepared yellow mustard (I sneak in some raw horseradish too,
    just a spoonful)
3/4 cup ketchup (or Craig's BBQ sauce)
3 tsps brown sugar
salt and pepper to taste

In a medium skillet, over medium heat, brown the ground beef, onion, and green pepper; drain off liquids. Stir in the garlic powder, mustard, ketchup, and brown sugar; mix thoroughly. Reduce heat, and simmer for 30 minutes. Season with salt and pepper.
Obviously, you can add a can of beer to the recipe, or any booze you'd like, honestly (whiskey is best, gin is worst), but be sure to add another 15-20 minutes to the cook time to get all that extra liquid cooked off, leaving only the power and the flavor.

BBQ CHICKEN

When you've got yourself a bottle of Craig's BBQ sauce, there really ain't nothing you can't make taste better, and that's a scientific fact. I'm telling you brother, next time you're whipping up a grilled cheese sandwich and washing it down with a Bloody Mary put yourself a dollop or two of Craig's into both. I bet you could mix that stuff with vanilla ice cream and make it taste pretty good, even if you gotta suck on some antacid when you're finished.

Now before this sounds too much like an advertisement, you remember what I said about Craig and his sauce, there's mojo in that stuff that can mix with what you're cooking to give it that extra kick.

As I am a big fan of chickens, slow cookers, and BBQ sauce, it would be like half a sin to put out this here book without adding all those ingredients together for something tasty. This recipe is especially useful if you are able to see a fight coming long enough in advance to sit down to this meal before the real horror show starts.

I've used this recipe a few times myself, with a few variations. Once I was down in south Florida working a case what I thought was going to be a two day bushwhack job on a gang of newbie worshippers of some fish god.

Turned out to be a hard-bitten coven of high priests running an Insmouth breeding scheme. They'd set up shop in a small town south of Jacksonville and were scooping up prostitutes and runaways, then throwing into the clutches of a few horny deep ones.

Apparently, the turnaround time on deep spawn is pretty short, and takes a lot out of the mamas, so after one or two rides on the icthio-merry-go-round, these poor girls were made into chum for their own hybrid babies. I'd picked up the trail and knew where the temple had been hidden, though in doing such an in-depth investigation I'd racked up a good bit of the darkness.

That is a constant danger during those cases that drag on. If you aren't able to get in and get out, you're liable to have to dive down into the deep to piece together the clues and strike the root. You read books that ought not to be read, you stare at symbols that make your soul hurt, you find yourself obsessing over photographs of the dead, and you start to wonder if you're chasing your own shadow. The real shitty part is that if the trail goes cold that's the sort of case that can haunt you the rest of your life, wondering what nightmare you couldn't uproot. You always wonder if you'd just overturned one more stone maybe you'd have found it. Or you do follow the trail of breadcrumbs, and you do find the house of horrors, and then after all the struggle to get there you've spent your strength and your sanity and you've got nothing left for the fight. That was back when I worked with Papa Proctor occasionally, before he became what he is today, and believe me he was spooky as hell, even back then.

A good slayer knows their own limitations, and there are times when no amount of shotguns or moonshine will get the job done. Sometimes you need a motherfucking sorcerer. Be careful what you ask for though, because the universe provides, and sometimes in spades. After I made contact, Proctor showed up a day later with two other hexers, voodoo boko types from Alabama, making me the odd man out real quick. They could see that I was already ate up with the darkness and in need of some serious cleansing, and the boko weren't going to make a play until I'd been dealt with. I couldn't blame 'em, as by then I'd taken to scratching symbols on the wall and couldn't help but hear the whispers of the dead girls in the photos I'd thumb tacked to the walls of my dingy little hotel room.

We drove out to an old campground, used to be a KOA or something, but shut down and never really repossessed by anybody. The boko lit up a bonfire, painted themselves and did one of the crazier dances I've ever seen, bringing down a spirit they called Papa Ogun into their bodies. One was the warrior and one the sorcerer, both the one spirit and both different. I had trouble following what they said, but I watched them slaughter the chickens right there, pluckin' 'em and throwin' 'em in the pot. Then they poured in sugar and rum, insisting that the god loved his sugar and his booze and if they held the vigil, the meal would both cleanse me and empower me.

We started around eight that night, and they made me and Proctor both get painted up and join the dance, and right at midnight, just as I was about to collapse (I wasn't a spring chicken even in my younger days), they declared the sacrament ready to consume. That was an important lesson for me, really earning my food, empowering the energy and nourishment of it by keeping a vigil, transforming it from meat and liquids into the literal food of the gods.

The sacrifice of the chickens was the cleansing part (and damn they was tasty) and the booze, though much of the actual liquid and sugar had cooked off, was the mojo.

We rolled heavy into that compound and brought them down in one of the most potent displays of hexing and shooting that I've ever participated in or even heard of since the Civil War days, and half of those are tall tales anyway.

1 whole chicken
1 (12 oz) bottle Craig's barbeque sauce
1/2 Italian Salad dressing
1/2 cup dark spiced rum
1/4 cup brown sugar

2 tblsps Worcestershire sauce

Place chicken in a slow cooker. Not everybody has the time or the education to pull a four hour dance vigil, and even then you'd kinda have to be a sorcerer more of the voodoo persuasion anyway. The slow cooker works just fine. In a bowl, mix the barbecue sauce, Italian salad dressing, brown sugar, rum and Worcestershire sauce. Pour over the chicken.
Cover, and cook 3 to 4 hours on High or 6 to 8 hours on Low.

CORNBREAD

Most southern meals just ain't complete without having yourself a wedge of cornbread to sop up all the leftover juices, gravy, and greasy goodness that escapes fork and spoon. Now while they say that God created men and Colt made them equal, the same can be said for butter.

No, I am not talking about what passes for butter on the shelves of retail black holes like Wal-Mart, Kroger, or wherever. I'm talking about real butter, straight from the churn. It's hard to get nowadays, but as with most things good and powerful in the culinary world, they can be found at some farmers markets if you've the coin to pay. If you can get handmade butter-milk, well, hell, let me know how I can get my hands on some.

Now, for you folks who really want to get serious about maximizing your mojo, find yourself some sprouted corn meal, as that's the closest thing you can get to the old maize. Folks used to worship corn gods, and for good reason, because corn used to be a super food. It had just about everything the body needed, but that was long before white men and GMOs. These days you've got to work hard to get corn to be anything more than starchy kernels that don't seem to do much but fill your belly and pass on through.

The old Aztecs used lime water alkaline solutions to break down the hull and release all the good stuff. These days we call it "nixtamalization". So, if you're feeling frisky, and have a whole day to spare to boil, treat, and hull the corn, then get yourself some homegrown corn and get to it. You, my friend, are going to be making some cornbread that will nuke the darkness right out of you, especially if you've already got those demons on the ropes with the main course.

I've seen Hershel and Andre grind corn that was treated like that, and while you'd think they'd make more cornbread, those boys are always munching on corn tortillas. When I say always, I'm saying it's like they're always nibbling on 'em the way other folks smoke cigarettes or chew gum, but when you deal with the darkness on a day to day basis the way those boys do, it makes a kind of sense. They live in Pine Bluff, another hellhole in Arkansas that is continuously befouled by the mythos. If it's not some upstart cult murdering prostitutes, it's some jumped up warlock trying to raise an army of shoggoth from the black water swamps that surround the place.

1/2 cup butter
2/3 cup white sugar
2 eggs
1 cup buttermilk
1/2 teaspoon baking soda
1 cup cornmeal
1 cup all-purpose flour
1/2 teaspoon salt
Preheat oven to 375 degrees F (175 degrees C).

Grease an 8 inch square pan. Melt butter in large skillet. Remove from heat and stir in sugar. Quickly add eggs and beat until well blended. Combine buttermilk with baking soda and stir into mixture in pan. Stir in cornmeal, flour, and salt until well blended and few lumps remain. Pour batter into the prepared pan. Bake in the preheated oven for 30 to 40 minutes, or until a toothpick inserted in the center comes out clean. I like to serve it up with real butter and a jar of molasses, which is how I was raised, though some folks do seem to prefer honey.

BEEF STROGANOFF

My dad wasn't the most adept cook in the world, though it wasn't as much from a lack of skill as it was a disinterest in all but a few recipes. He had his moments of complexity, though typically those were not expressed in the kitchen. That was my mama's domain and he was a man of his time, so was content to leave her to her culinary kingdom. However, there were a few dishes that he was famous for, at least to those happy few who were guests at our table here and there over the years.

Beef Stroganoff was his signature dish, though being a dyed in the wool southern man, he stayed true to his immigrant roots in his own way and this was one of them. The other was keeping a small plaque that held the Clan Munro coat of arms, our Scottish ancestors from the old country.

As a rule, I don't prepare this meal just for any old cleansing. I whip this one up if it's been one of those kinds of close calls where you almost lost not just your own life, but the life of someone you really care about. Hard as we slayers try to be, there's always that human connection, with your comrades in arms or your family or maybe just the family that lives down the road.

When the grasping darkness has tried to tear away those you love, and you've beaten it back, that is a certain kind of horror show that plays out in the back of your head every time you see those people. You envision what 'could have' happened. Even though you did win, it's like a whole second fight, and it's the sort that is insidious in its subtlety. It'll creep into you, and you've got to root it out. Whomever it is that you're wanting to give thanks for having, and keeping, in your life, that's when you want to throw some beef stroganoff down your gullet.

1 pound cubed beef stew meat
1 (10.75 ounce) can condensed golden mushroom soup
1/2 cup chopped onion
1 tblsp Worcestershire sauce
1/4 cup water
4 ozs. cream cheese

In a slow cooker, combine the meat, soup, onion, Worcestershire sauce and water. You could get real hardcore and cook this thing the old way, which is to uncover and stir about every hour, adding just a tiny splash of red wine every time you do. Don't want to overdo the wine, but it adds a good flavor, some extra mojo, and a touch of liquid to replace what's lost each time you uncover the pot.

This is an important enough dish that I do it the old way, and that hourly attention becomes a meditation of its own, and Lord knows I take a pull or two from the bottle while I'm doing it. Dang, now that I'm thinking about it, I've probably drank more marsala wine than most folks, seeing as how about half goes in the food and half goes in me while I'm cooking.

Cook on low setting for 8 hours, or on high setting for about 5 hours. Same applies whether you're doing it on the stove or in a slow cooker. Stir in cream cheese just before serving, or if you aren't a fan of cream cheese you can pour in cottage cheese. My dad used cream cheese when he had it, cottage cheese when he had it, even cheese curds if that's all there was, though most of the time honestly he used heavy cream, as we were kinda poor and in those days fancy dairy could be tough to come by.

STICKY CHICKEN

Have you noticed yet, how I haven't included any recipes that involve anything that lives in the water? There's a reason my friend, and it ain't a pretty one. The horrors of the mythos are creatures of extreme 'otherness', and the realm from which they wake is deep and dark.

The magic of the world often expresses or manifests itself in a sort of symbolic way, where things have correspondence, and all the puzzle pieces fit together in a robust, but still delicate, way, just like cooking, which is why being mindful of what you are doing is so important. You can see it reflected in the world around you, and it all starts to make a terrible kind of sense.

On the briny shores and lonely islands of salt water oceans, the cults of Dagon call up nightmares from the crushing black of the abyss, and on the slippery banks of rivers and swamps there are madmen and backwater clans who awaken terrible, hungry things from the primordial soup.

That's just two examples, but you're starting to see my point right?

You can't trust meat that comes from the water, because that is Their realm. Be it a tasty sea bass or a plate of boiled crawfish, none of it is ever going to be fully safe. That's not to say that those creatures are inherently evil or anything, it's just that they live in the world of our enemies, they are creatures of the watery realm that live in the shadow of the darkness from birth to death, generation after generation. They sometimes carry spells, disease, and nightmares from the depths, woven into the very fabric of their being and hidden within their flesh. Sometimes they are the nightmares. That's why I gave up fishing, much as it saddened me to do so.

I was out in my little flat bottom boat, doing a spot of fishing in an oxbow lake maybe ten miles from my place down in Louisiana. Nothing special, just out looking for an afternoon of cold beers and maybe a fresh catfish dinner. I'd only been working as a slayer for a few years, and most of the action I'd seen was cult psychos, so when my rod went wild I didn't think anything of it.

At first.

I set the hook and started reeling whatever it was in. That's when it pulled on the line so hard that I lost my grip on the rod at the same time the line snapped free. I could see heavy movement in the water up ahead and I knew I was in trouble. I've seen big catfish in my day, some large alli-gators and even a few of the gar fish that haunt the dams, but whatever this was took the cake. I only caught a glimpse of it before it went all the way down. From what I could see, it looked like a cross between an octopus and a giant catfish. Though I was new to the game, I was enough of a slayer to know when I was facing down one of... them.

I reacted as fast as I could, and put a few clouds of buckshot where last I'd seen the creature. I turned the boat around and sped out of there as fast as my little motor would take me. The water was nearly seven feet deep, and I wasn't about to tangle with that thing on its own turf. It attacked the boat twice, though, thankfully, I had brought my machete with me and was able to hack at its tentacles so that it couldn't get a firm enough grip to flip the boat. Eventually it gave up the chase and I was able to get out of the swamp.

As soon as I was home I called up a few slayer buddies and we started looking for clues as to who brought up that creature. That's one of those things that a lot of slayers still don't seem to have figured out. Lots of these monsters are already manifested in our world, because they've been here since the beginning and never left. They just went to sleep, and lay dreaming until some son of a bitch comes along and wakes 'em up.
Where there are monsters there are also evil men, every time. Ignorance and lack of understanding is pretty damn common amongst the mythos cults, especially the redneck gangs that plague the American south. Lots of times they'll stumble on some ancient dead name, or figure out three fourths of a badass spell, and they'll end up summoning or awakening a monster.

I know it's really just an academic point, but this here is a book of knowledge, so you might as well learn. A monster is just a monster, and it doesn't become a shoggoth until the Will of a Master it set upon it. Lots of these backwater groups are operating on half-truths and tall tales passed down by word of mouth; maybe some semi-literate family leader wrote something in a notebook at best. So, these groups usually end up worshipping the very monster they summon or awaken, whereas more knowledgeable (and deadly) cults and warlocks will be able to transform a monster into a full-blown shoggoth.

I see it like this, a monster is really just a hungry battle tank made out of meat, which is dangerous enough, but when you put the mind of a powerful badass behind the wheel, then you're in trouble. Next time you're fighting a gang of rednecks who worship some swampy octopus monster, consider yourself lucky that those poor bastards didn't know better. The point I'm making, and I know I get long winded sometimes, is that you can't trust meat that comes from the water. Eat what strides the land, grows in the dirt, or soars in the sky, but if it breathes water, steer well clear, because even if that fish ain't a monster its likely set it eyes on one monster or another, and sometimes that's all it takes.

Needless to say Cajun cooking includes a ton of water creatures, but as I've discussed before, that kind of cooking is all about fighting fire with fire

4 tsps salt
2 tsps paprika
1 tsp onion powder
1 tsp dried thyme
1 tsp white pepper
1/2 tsp cayenne pepper
1/2 tsp black pepper
1/2 tsp garlic powder
2 onions, quartered
2 (4 pound) whole chickens

In a small bowl, mix together salt, paprika, onion powder, thyme, white pepper, black pepper, cayenne pepper, and garlic powder. Remove and discard giblets from chicken. Usually, I'd say leave all those extra calories and flavor in the dish, but in this case we're trying to remove some of that 'chicken fat' taste and let the spices do the real work, so I remove them. Rinse chicken cavity, and pat dry with paper towel. Rub each chicken inside and out with spice mixture. Place 1 onion into the cavity of each chicken.

Place chickens in a re-sealable bag or double wrap with plastic wrap.

Refrigerate overnight, or at least 4 to 6 hours, not everybody likes to let it set over night, but I like preparing food with the assumption that I'm going to survive whatever hell I'm about to walk into and come home to eat it. Plus it tastes better. Preheat oven to 250 degrees F (120 degrees C).Place chickens in a roasting pan. Bake uncovered for 5 hours, to a minimum internal temperature of 180 degrees F (85 degrees C). Let the chickens stand for 10 minutes before carving.

SALISBURY STEAK

This is one of those robust and flavorful kinds of meals with a sort of power that is just as much about cooking as it is about eating and cleansing. In this recipe I have your basic condensed French onion soup, but if you really want to make this thing right you've got to make the soup yourself before adding it to the steak recipe.

I don't have a particular recipe, as it were, for French onion soup, as I usually make it on the go in someone else's kitchen (same with the steak recipe), but in general, it's some beef or venison stock, chopped onions, olive or vegetable oil, and whatever kinds of spices are handy. Brown the onions then chuck everything else into the skillet until its boiling, then reduce heat and let it simmer for maybe twenty minutes.

Some folks strain out the onions, but I like it chunky, so leave em in. Once you have the soup, you let that sit while you put together the rest of the dish, then add it in when the time comes. This is a good recipe for groups, in addition to being great for that kind of meditation-in-the-work kind of cooking that sets your mind and soul up for the cleansing that's coming when you finally chow down.

1 (10.5 oz) can condensed French onion soup
1 1/2 pounds ground beef
1/2 cup dry bread crumbs
1 egg

1/4 tsp salt
1/8 tsp ground black pepper
1 tblsp all purpose flour
1/4 cup ketchup
1/4 cup water
1 tblsp Worcestershire sauce
1/2 tsp mustard powder

In a large bowl, mix together 1/3 cup condensed French onion soup with ground beef, bread crumbs, egg, salt and black pepper. Shape into 6 oval patties. The way I see it you've got to put so much effort into this dish that you might as well get yourself either a dinner for the whole gang or set your-self up for some leftovers.

In a large skillet, over medium-high heat, brown both sides of patties. Pour off excess fat. If you are an enterprising sort of person then all that tasty excess is going to get put to good use in the form of a fine brown gravy, to be poured over mashed potatoes or a venison steak. In a small bowl, blend flour and remaining soup until smooth. Mix in ketchup, water, Worcestershire sauce and mustard powder. Pour over meat in skillet. Cover, and cook for 20 minutes, stirring occasionally.

MACARONI AND CHEESE

If there ever was a king of comfort food, it would be macaroni and cheese. Whether you're buying the pre-packaged chemical powder kind for ninety cents or you're homemaking the real-deal good stuff, it is a magical meal. From crying children, to disgruntled adults, to the hospitality of strangers, mixing up some cheesiness into a heap of buttery pasta is an act that has power.

You're telling your waistline that it can shut up and sit down. You're telling the world that it can hold on a minute while you enjoy yourself. You're telling yourself that you deserve a tasty meal that has very little in the way of nutrition, but all kinds of flavor.

Mac and cheese is a paradox that way, in that it is somewhat empty of physical value, but supercharged with meaning and mojo. Nobody ever made a bowl of macaroni and cheese for someone they didn't care about at least a little bit. Skeptical? Go ahead, think about it for just a moment, and I defy you to tell me about a time someone slammed some mac and cheese down in front of you without at least a little care.

The dish itself is bone-head simple, just a bowl of pasta with some cheese sauce, and really that's all it takes, but the preparation is the key for the slayer looking to maximize the power of the dish. You can throw together some pre-fab mac and cheese and it'll take the edge off, but if you really want to soothe someone's soul (or your own for that soothing of others), hand making as much as possible is the way to go.

Macaroni and cheese has little to no value as a magical dish if you're just making it for yourself. It's almost like the universe decided that it was something that had to be made for others in order to have power, and as such it is the one dish that I've ever heard of that will cleanse you without you ever putting a bite in your mouth, so long as you prepared the dish yourself and did it with light and love in your heart.

Sounds hippy-dippy, but believe me, pilgrim, it's true as the north star.

You can't even serve someone you're pissed at a bowl of the stuff without getting a little boost. Making this dish on your own, from scratch, gives you the kind of cleansing that keeps you going against the worst of the horrors of the mythos.

The one man I've ever met in person, who has seen the Thing in the Moonlight and not only lived to tell the tale, but did so with sanity and academic acumen, was--well, shit, there's no way I'm going to name his name. The man is still alive and I owe it to keep him off the books. Guys like me and Fix are good out front, but this guy is a be-hind the curtain sort of chap. Suffice it to say, he was a well-learned man, and in our world that carries a risk all its own. He saw IT, and happened to drag his quivering self to a kitchen (he never said where) and proceeded to whip up a tasty meal of macaroni and cheese and pan-fried green beans for an unsuspecting family.

 Truth be told, I think he actually broke into the house of a stranger and held them at gunpoint, but even then, mac and cheese is good, and serving to his sorta-kinda hostages kept his mind together long enough for him to get out of town with his skin and his sanity.

 Do for others, and the mac and cheese will do for you.

This here is my own recipe for baked macaroni and cheese, and honestly there's a thousand ways to make it. I'm just showing you how I like to do it.

1 (8 oz) package elbow macaroni
1 (8 oz) package shredded sharp Cheddar cheese
1 (12 oz) container small curd cottage cheese
1 (8 oz) container sour cream
1/4 cup grated Parmesan cheese
salt and pepper to taste
1 cup dry bread crumbs

1/4 cup butter, melted

Preheat oven to 350 degrees. Bring a large pot of lightly salted water to a boil, add pasta, and cook until done; drain. In 9x13 inch baking dish, stir together macaroni, shredded Cheddar cheese, cottage cheese, sour cream, Parmesan cheese, salt and pepper. In a small bowl, mix together bread crumbs and melted butter. Sprinkle topping over macaroni mixture. Bake 30 to 35 minutes, or until top is golden. Serve it to folks you at least sorta give a shit about, and it'll do the trick. The more you love 'em the more potent the power will be.

BISCUITS

You are no kinda cook if you can't whip up a mess o' biscuits. Not only are they tasty on their own, but they're great for sopping up all those extra tidbits of whatever dish you're making. I like to pour white gravy over mine, but there are purists out there who won't even touch one without molasses.

Biscuits are also one of the little signals folks in the loose slayer network use to give each other a hand. When I say loose network, I mean loose. I barely know a dozen slayers who are alive and kicking as of this writing, though there's always them as don't get noticed, by me or anybody else. There's other groups that I don't know about who don't know about me and mine. Keeps us decentralized and damn hard to wipe out. That's part of what's kept us in the fight this long.

However, because of the transitory nature of our work, even those of us who have a permanent home put a lot of miles under our wheels, and sometimes you need help from a stranger. It's tough to trust, even between slayers. To help with this, there are those who feel a calling to set up way stations. I've talked about this a little before, there's a whole other network of truck stops that dot the country, following the old ley lines of ages past, like Highway 66, or the coast drive on Pacific 1, or the pig trail that winds its way through the Ozarks.

If I'm looking to receive help or maybe offer it up, I pull over at a truck stop and try the biscuits. I mean real truck stops too, by the way, like TA Travel Centers or Love's, not one of those Exxon or Valero knock offs. A stop that has hot biscuits 24 hours a day, showers, beds, and a bona fide trucker's lounge. You pull in, have yourself a biscuit, and if its packing the mojo then you know you've got a friend working the kitchen.

Like I said, trust is hard won, a good plate of biscuits and gravy ain't a partnership, but it does mean a safe place to shower and bed down for the night, knowing that there's a slayer in the house keeping watch. Sad to say, there's fewer and fewer of them out there, our numbers rise and fall through the generations, and unfortunately we're waiting pretty hard these days.

Still, a warm biscuit with just enough mojo to clear away the cobwebs that always creep out of your subconscious on those long hauls is a beautiful thing.

2 cups all-purpose flour
1 tblsp baking powder
1 tsp salt
1 tblsp white sugar
1/3 cup shortening
1 cup milk

Preheat oven to 425 degrees. I'm a good cook, and I have my way of making my biscuits, but every place is different, so you really gotta let the flavor wash over you to get the full effect. I use hemp milk instead of cow's milk, partly because I prefer the taste and partly because dammit it's just healthier. Call me a hippie if you gotta, but my hemp biscuits will set you right as rain on a sunny day.

In a large bowl, whisk together the flour, baking powder, salt, and sugar. Cut in the shortening until the mixture resembles coarse meal. Gradually stir in milk until dough pulls away from the side of the bowl. Turn out onto a floured surface, and knead 15 to 20 times. Pat or roll dough out to 1 inch thick. Cut biscuits with a large cutter or juice glass dipped in flour. Repeat until all dough is used. Brush off the excess flour, and place biscuits onto an ungreased baking sheet. Bake for 13 to 15 minutes in the preheated oven, or until edges begin to brown. You can do all this on a campfire too, if you grease up a good sized dutch oven and place your dough carefully in a spiral pattern around the inside of the oven. I do enjoy me some campfire cooking, especially when I'm on a hunt, be that for shoggoth, cultists, or just a stout buck for my deep freeze.

FRENCH TOAST

There's an old trick that my daddy taught me to keeping yourself going just a little longer when you're in the world and basically broke. You head into a local diner and order hot water in a bowl, usually cost you maybe fifty cents. Then you stir in the complimentary ketchup packets and have yourself some tomato soup along with the complimentary saltine crackers. You'll get some weird looks, but it beats going hungry.

In that realm of thinking, I wanted to talk about French toast. There is a delicate art to making French toast and this recipe ain't it. You can pick up any number of cooking magazines or gourmet cookbooks and find delicate variations on this particularly decadent breakfast food. They'll talk about keeping a low heat, not allowing the egg to run too much and create a foot, and then whole other bits about making the cinnamon and butter and egg batter. They'll even go into what kinds of powdered sugar work best. Those are all good ways, and they yield fantastic meals, though what I'm looking to do with my French toast recipe is feed a gang of hungry killers using stale bread and a campfire.

We all have those times in our life when money is short, sometimes real damn short, and this is a good way to feed yourself and your buds if you find yourself needing to save your extra cash for gas and bullets. More than once in my life, and likely in yours, the heat from local law enforcement is a little too much, and cooling my heels camping in the woods for a few weeks before re-surfacing has been the smart move. When you're in that kind of situation there ain't much in the way of fine fare, but with a few loaves of old bread and some cheap eggs, you can cook up a feast that'll make your time spent in hiding a little less grim.

1/4 cup all-purpose flour
1 cup milk (or you can use a handful of complimentary creamers)
1 pinch salt
3 eggs (or powdered eggs if that's what you've got)
1/2 tsp ground cinnamon (coffee shops have this complimentary usually)
1 tblsp white sugar (about 1 packet of sugar)
12 thick slices bread (day old, or even week old will do)

Measure flour into a large mixing bowl, whatever is handy. Slowly whisk in the milk with a fork, unless you're the sort to have an emergency whisk (don't laugh, some do). Whisk in the salt, eggs, cinnamon, and sugar until smooth.
Heat a lightly oiled griddle or frying pan over medium heat, in other words,

get your pan on a good bed of coals, let that heat envelope the pan instead of assaulting it the way flames would. Soak bread slices in egg mixture until saturated, that's where the real magick comes from, especially if you happen to have just a touch of booze to spice it up (especially fireball whiskey, hoowee, that makes for some fine French-toast-on-the-dodge. Cook bread on each side until golden brown. Serve hot.

VENISON STEW

I haven't spoken much about hunting for food as much as I've talked about slaying monsters, but I reckon that if you're reading this, then you know at least a thing or two about how to do yourself some living off the land.

Every redneck worth his boots knows how to hunt deer, bait a hook, and coax a few crops out of this hard earth. This here recipe is for the boys back home, as it were. Anything you can make with beef, you can make with venison, and though it's game meat, its leaner and, in a lot of ways, more honest meat. There is great power in the consuming of flesh that you've killed yourself.

One of the great tragedies of our growing population and the reliance upon massive agriculture and livestock industries is that we don't take a hand in the killing and claiming of our meat. Most of us just shell out the dollars for it and don't think about the animal whose blood used to pump through those tissues. Sure, I know that venison tastes like dirt, if dirt was meat, and that no manner of spice or sauce is gonna make deer meat ever taste as good as a cut of real Kobe beef. The important thing here is, that even if it doesn't taste as good, the venison has an honest taste to it, and the power of the stag rests within. You take an animal from the wild, claim its life by your own hand in the hunt, then according to many you and that animal have shared something, and when you eat it, the beast's power flows into you. Combine that with the kind of arcane cooking we're doing as slayers, and you've got yourself the kind of food that fuels heroes. If you really feel like being a cynical asshole about everything I just said, then remember this, a deer will cost you the price of a bullet for more meat than you can carry comfortably, and sometimes that's the steepest price you can afford.

This here is another camping kind of recipe, the idea being that you'll want to cut up and cook your deer as soon as possible after you've killed it, while the meat is still warm from the life that was burning within. As such you'll want to have a buddy with you for this dish, so he or she can get the fire going, prep the kitchen area, and be pre-pared for you to come walking out of the bush, game in hand.

2 pounds stew meat, cut into 1 inch cubes
1/4 cup all purpose flour
1/2 tsp salt
1/2 tsp ground black pepper
1 clove garlic, minced
1 bay leaf
1 tsp paprika
1 tsp Worcestershire sauce
1 onion, chopped
1 1/2 cups beef broth
3 potatoes, diced

4 carrots, sliced
1 stalk celery, chopped

Cut yourself two thick strips of meat from the haunches, once you've skinned and gutted the kill. Get those two strips on the fire right away, preferably on a wooden spit (just whittle a branch and spear the meat, hold it over the flames). Roast the strips for just a few minutes, until the top layer is good and seared and chow down. It will be greasy, and some folks might claim you'll get worms or something.

Ignore all of that. This is a sacred thing you're doing.

You've flame-kissed the first cuts of a fresh kill, which captures and forms the energy of those intense moments of life and death. That little ritual will not only get you fed and cleansed right away, but it empowers the rest of the meat, and that energetic charge will stay infused in the meat, even if you throw it in a deep freeze (which is very likely, and a big part of what makes this ritual so important).

For the stew, which is the second part of the ritual, you'll be standing a vigil around that fire for another 10 hours or so. Might not seem worth it at first, but once you taste the stew, its gonna make you smile, and again, this is a ritual that makes the entire harvest of meat empowered and long-lasting.

Place meat into a pot, and then hang it on a camp iron over the fire (up if it's flame, lower if it's just coals). In a small bowl, mix together, the flour, salt, and pepper; pour over meat and stir to coat meat with flour mixture. Stir in the garlic, bay leaf, paprika, Worcestershire sauce, onion, vegetable broth, potatoes, carrots, and celery.

Cover, and cook for 10 to 12 hours. Keep a bottle of cheap red wine on hand so that you can replace the liquids as they cook off. After the whole thing is done you should have a very thick stew that mostly tastes of venison and carrots, with a distinct red wine after-taste that hits the spot just right.

SHEPHERD'S PIE

America is, other than a very small slice of the population, a nation of immigrants, and our food reflects that.

Here in the South, a great many of the past-times, values, religions, and culinary traditions ended up sticking around once those hearty pioneers had transformed themselves into locals. Their ways combined with the natives, mixed with other immigrants, and all came together on the hard edge of the frontier to form unique patchwork cultures of their very own. The great clans of the Appalachians are the most famous of these, followed by the Cajun folks down in Louisiana. There are a great many, if far less famous, communities spread out across the south, holed up in the Ozark mountains, the White river valley, the scrublands of south Texas, and little enclaves all over Kentucky, Virginia, and Tennessee. They're everywhere, and many folks don't even see the effect that such things have had. Things cross borders, and everyone gets a taste. Cajun cooking, for example follows its roots to France, and Parisians get to taste the spice of the Louisiana swamps in their street cafes.

In our case, for this particular recipe, the hearty shepherd of the Scottish highlands and his calorie-packed pie has found its way onto the menus of Americans descended from the first Scots to cross over. Maybe one day they'll serve fried catfish and black-eyed peas with cornbread to people in Glasgow. Our food makes us stronger, and when we expand our palate we are also expanding our awareness, our influence, and broadening our power.

Now, you can imagine how bored of that speech I was by the time old Alan Cleggain finally spooned a helping of pie onto my plate. I had already put four men in the ground that day, and the mud and the blood was still caked on my boots. I was in no mood for that much talk, but it set the stage for the first taste, and just like he said, I could taste the history, the journey, and felt my own struggles being set against a backdrop of pioneer courage.

You will too.

4 large potatoes, peeled and cubed
1 tblsp butter
1 tblsp finely chopped onion
1/4 cup shredded Cheddar cheese
salt and pepper to taste
5 carrots, chopped
1 tblsp vegetable oil
1 onion, chopped
1 pound lean ground beef
2 tblsps all purpose flour
1 tblsp ketchup
3/4 cup beef broth
1/4 cup shredded Cheddar cheese

Bring a large pot of salted water to a boil. Add potatoes and cook until tender, but still firm, about 15 minutes. Drain and mash. Mix in butter, finely chopped onion and 1/4 cup shred-ded cheese. Season with salt and pepper to taste; set aside.

Bring a large pot of salted water to a boil. Add carrots and cook until tender, but still firm, about 15 minutes. Drain, mash and set aside.

Preheat oven to 375 degrees. Heat oil in a large frying pan. Add onion and cook until clear. Add ground beef and cook until well browned. Pour off excess fat, then stir in flour and cook 1 minute. Add ketchup and beef broth. Bring to a boil, reduce heat and simmer for 5 minutes. Spread the ground beef in an even layer on the bottom of a 2 quart casserole dish. Next, spread a layer of mashed carrots. Top with the mashed potato mixture and sprinkle with remaining shredded cheese.

Bake in the preheated oven for 20 minutes, or until golden brown.

GREEN BEAN CASSEROLE

There are monsters that lurk in the angles between our perceptions. They are powerful beyond measure, ancient and unknowable, and today we're gonna fight 'em with a casserole.

Dairy and plants of the earth all mixed up and baked to make a dish that's damn near a meal on its own.

It's important to remember that when we are in the kitchen, we're fighting the good fight just as much as we are when we're hip deep in tentacles and breathing gunsmoke. The darkness that takes root inside us when we fight the mythos is a cunning force, and it begins to work against us the moment we first witness the horrors of the world behind the world. It will work to make us apathetic about cleansing ourselves after an engagement, or work to put little obstacles in our way, the hell of minor inconveniences as it were.

All too often there is a near overwhelming urge to just throw a TV dinner in the microwave and forget about it. It's hard to come back and dive right into preparing and cooking a meal be-fore you've had a chance to clean up, because you've got to get to it right away. This is why myself and most everyone I know drink while we cook, because it lets us keep a hex handy and ourselves armored up during the time it takes to get the cleansing ready to perform.

This is a simple casserole that I like to whip up on those days when finding the motivation is extra hard, mostly because you can just put this together and throw it in the oven while you pound a few drinks and fire up the grill maybe. I use cast iron skillets, deep dish style, so after I do all my skillet work I just put the cast iron in the oven. Try not to fill up on the Ritz crackers, okay? They don't cleanse for shit unless they're part of a good recipe.

2 tblsps butter
2 tblsps all purpose flour
1 tsp salt
1 tsp white sugar
1/4 cup onion, diced
1 cup sour cream
3 (14.5 oz) cans French style green beans, drained
2 cups shredded Cheddar cheese
1/2 cup crumbled buttery round crackers
1 tblsp butter, melted

Preheat oven to 350 degrees and melt 2 tablespoons butter in a large skillet over medium heat. Stir in flour until smooth, and cook for one minute. Stir in the salt, sugar, onion, and sour cream. Add green beans, and stir to coat. Spread shredded cheese over the top. In a small bowl, toss together cracker crumbs and remaining butter, and sprinkle over the cheese. Bake for 25 minutes in the preheated oven, or until the top is golden and cheese is bubbly.

COLESLAW

With all of the high calorie meals we've been wolfing down, with all that gravy, butter, and grease, we're going to need something to cut that fatty taste and cleanse the palate.
Enter coleslaw.

It's like a reset button for your mouth. Let's say you've just put back three huge pieces of fried catfish and you're still really hungry, but there's just too much fried goodness happening and your taste buds need a break. That's when you help yourself to a few forkfuls of coleslaw. Not only does it cut through fat mouth, but it tastes great too. After a few bites you'll find that the next piece of catfish, fried chicken, fried pickles, oysters Rockefeller, or whatever you're working on, is going to taste so much better than it did the first time.

Every hero needs a sidekick, and coleslaw is good at the job. Bringing food to every event is big in the South, be it weddings, funerals, parties, or whatever, and most slayers who work together and cook together have a sort of informal tradition that whom-ever is hosting the gang makes the coleslaw. That's part of our symbolic way of observing the rule of hospitality, which is a deep magic.

If you allow someone into your home, you are taking them under your protection, they must be courteous, respectful, and trustworthy. They say that the old faerie folk came up with the rule of hospitality. Others say it's the way of all gods and spirits, and Lord knows all manner of beings and powers follow-ed folk as they settled the south.

There's reasons for southern hospitality being some-what legendary, be-cause down here the rule of hospitality still has power, even if not everyone knows about it. The slayer who is taking others under his protection makes the coleslaw as a gesture of assistance, a show of support. The culinary equivalent of saying, "I've got your back, so make your move partner," is setting out a big bowl of fresh cole-slaw at a potluck of supernatural badasses.

1 (16 oz) bag coleslaw mix
2 tblsps diced onion
2/3 cup creamy salad dressing (such as Miracle Whip)
3 tblsps vegetable oil
1/2 cup white sugar
1 tblsp white vinegar
1/4 tsp salt
1/2 tsp poppy seeds

Combine the coleslaw mix and onion in a large bowl. Whisk together, the salad dressing, vegetable oil, sugar, vinegar, salt, and poppy seeds in a medium bowl; blend thoroughly. Pour dressing mixture over coleslaw mix and toss to coat. You can chill it for a few hours if you want, but personally

I like to get it out there for folks to eat as soon as I've made it.

PEACH COBBLER

In the way that apple pie is a tasty cleansing dessert and potent shoggoth bait all in one, peach cobbler is a hell of a treat that pulls double duty as creating a temporary weird, magnetic effect on those who eat an empowered piece. I can't explain why it works this way, but there's been enough stories circulating around the slayer underground that it's not so easy to dismiss. Theories abound, but like with most things in this funky world, I go with what works and don't worry so much about the how's and why's, cuz that road only gets you to the padded cell that much faster.

What I know is this. When you put away a piece of peach cobbler made by someone powerful (which is pretty much all slayers and sorcerers) then for a short time you become something akin to a vortex for weird occurrences. If there's something strange going on nearby, then once that cobbler magick is in you, that strange will get on your shoes by the time you've digested the food.

Now, I know this sounds like it's the nuclear bomb in the slayer's investigative arsenal, but before you think it's the super-tool for just walking into random towns and having cobbler that will make all the cultists reveal themselves to you, you're dead wrong. When I say strangeness, I mean everything, not just the mythos. You could find yourself being knighted by a homeless man who has decided he is King Arthur, or you could find one of those alleyways with an entrance that is also the exit, or maybe you'll just see some weird faces in windows and wonder if you just saw a handful of ghosts. However, for every nine times you pull this trick and end up encountering something strange, but ultimately innocuous, there will be that one that uncovers mythos activity.

Ever heard of the Black Dahlia murder? That's how they found her body out in that vacant lot in Los Angeles back in the 40's. Officially the case went unsolved, though occult lore has it that while the police chased down bogus leads and perverted socialites, a few hardboiled slayers slugged it out all brass-knuckles and revolvers against tentacles and teeth with a powerfully entrenched Cthulhu cult that had nearly taken over the Hollywood film industry. Nothing anyone will ever read about in the papers, of course, but they got the job done, and it all started with a piece of peach cobbler.

This is a ton of work that might only end up in you discovering nothing more dangerous than the local conspiracy theorist. Then again, it could crack open the case of a lifetime.

Oh, and one last warning, when you open yourself up to the strange, you never know what form it will take, and even if it's not mythos it could be dangerous. This is a risky move, which is why folks don't use it, for the most part, unless they are coming up dry on leads with every other method.

Filling:

8 fresh peaches - peeled, pitted and sliced into thin wedges
1/4 cup white sugar
1/4 cup brown sugar
1/4 tsp ground cinnamon
1/8 tsp ground nutmeg
1 tsp fresh lemon juice
2 tsps cornstarch

Crust:
1 cup all-purpose flour
1/4 cup white sugar
1/4 cup brown sugar
1 teaspoon baking powder
1/2 tsp salt
6 tblsps unsalted butter, chilled and cut into small pieces
1/4 cup boiling water

Mix Together:
3 tblsps white sugar
1 tsp ground cinnamon

Preheat oven to 425 degrees F (220 degrees C). In a large bowl, combine peaches, 1/4 cup white sugar, 1/4 cup brown sugar, 1/4 teaspoon cinnamon, nutmeg, lemon juice, and cornstarch.

Toss to coat evenly, and pour into a 2 quart baking dish. Bake in preheated oven for 10 minutes.

Be sure to have yourself a cocktail while you work, you're gonna need it. Meanwhile, in a large bowl, combine flour, 1/4 cup white sugar, 1/4 cup brown sugar, baking powder, and salt. Blend in butter with your fingertips, or a pastry blender, until mixture resembles coarse meal. Stir in water until just combined. Remove peaches from oven, and drop spoonfuls of topping over them. Sprinkle entire cobbler with the sugar and cinnamon mixture. Bake until topping is golden, about 30 minutes.

CHITTERLINGS

Now, I know I said you can't go doing much with pork other than a pinch of salt and a touch of flame, and I wasn't lying, but I tell you what, nothing says 'step away from the darkness and come get a hug' like a plate of piping hot chitlin's. Enough folks call em chitterlings that I titled it that in this book, but not once in my life have I heard a slayer from Arkansas or Louisiana call 'em that. Still, I figure best to keep things on the broad stroke, so chitterlings it is.

Like some of the hunting rituals we hold for dear, the same sort of practice is held during the slaughter of swine by those who keep the old ways. You won't get much in the way of cleansing out of that chitterlings plate though, as I've said, the pig is a special sort of beast. However, if you keep the custom, there's a bond and a magick of a kind that is raised and shared with the folks who participate.

When you treat the animal with respect, honor its sacrifice, and share in the slaughter, then all of that meat is exceptionally empowered. Slicing and frying up those intestines as soon as they are removed, which ought to be right after the pig has been hung and bled, in the company of like-minded people, will move a lot of that mojo around and further forge the binds of community, camaraderie, and family.

10 pounds frozen cleaned chitterlings, thawed
1 onion, roughly chopped
2 tsps salt
1 tsp crushed red pepper flakes
1 tsp minced garlic

Soak the chitterlings in cold water throughout the cleaning stage, preferably with some salt. I like to use pink sea salt for mine, gives 'em a little extra kick. Each chitterling should be examined and run under cold water, all foreign materials should be removed and discarded, because let's face it, the pig can digest things you can't.

Chitterlings should retain some fat, so be careful to leave some on, lord knows we ain't eating this stuff for our health, so leave the good stuff where you find it. After each chitterling has been cleaned, soak in two cold water baths for a few minutes. The second water should be clearer. If not, soak in one more bath. If you gotta do a third, then do it, but with most hand-raised pigs, where the beast has lived a beast's life and not been kept up in some hellish pen, then the double soak ought to get the job done. Place the chitterlings in a 6 quart pot and fill with cold water. Bring to a rolling boil, and then add the onion and season with salt, garlic and red pepper flakes. Continue to simmer for 3 to 4 hours, depending on how tender you like them, and since they tend to be a bit chewy, I'd venture a guess that you'd like 'em real tender if you're new to the food. I like to eat mine along with a plate of collard greens, maybe some fried potatoes, and lots of malt vinegar, though some folks like hot sauce or even salsa.

POLK SALAD

In some parts of the South you can take paper grocery bags out into the sunnier patches of woods, even groves that ain't all that wild, and find large leafy greens that most folks call polk salad. From what I hear that's just a country word for 'poor man's salad'. I grew up thinking it was a kind of cruel joke that if those greens were the salad that poor folks get to eat, it seems mean that we have to boil our leaves or they'll make you sick, whereas a rich man's salad has all kinds of stuff you can eat just as it comes.

As I kid, I guess I thought raw meant fancy. For many people, for many years, polk salad was one of the few vegetables that they were able to reliably get their hands on, especially during hard times, which for some folks in this great nation is all the damn time. Now that I'm older, I still go pick a few sacks of polk salad when I happen to be home, just to keep myself honest. It's a lot of work for not much of a meal, but there's a connectivity to it that should not be overlooked.

It's a plant that grows wild all on its own, with no touch of man's hand to affect its path. It grows when and where it likes, no matter what anyone tells you. It is an unpredictable plant that grows when such suits it, and stays hidden when such suits it. Finding a patch is like a blessing from the forest, and if you pick it and cook it with respect, then partner, that polk salad will reveal itself to be the absolute most cleansing dish a slayer can get in their bellies, short of tackling a deer and breaking its neck with your bare hands, and even then this is a powerful second.

Now, the plant that we call polk salad is slightly different than its domesticated relative, the collard green, but honestly, they look and taste the same, only difference is the mojo, and for us that's the one that matters. Good polk salad will take a harrowing journey through the underbelly of this bloody dark world and wash it so well that the memory of it will feel more like having been to a really scary movie. It won't stop the nightmares, or the creeping madness, but nothing will, so you might as well have a plate of greens and keep going for just another day, because another day is about all you can hope for.

1 1/2 quarts water
1 pound of fatty meat (beef, chicken, venison, any cut with a little fat on it)

4 pounds of greens, rinsed and trimmed (takes a lot just to make a little)
1/2 tsp crushed red pepper flakes
1/4 cup vegetable oil
salt and pepper to taste

Place the water and the fatty meat in a large pot with a tight-fitting lid. Bring to a boil. Lower the heat to very low and simmer covered for 30 minutes. Add the greens and the hot pepper flakes the pot. Simmer covered for about 2 hours, stirring occasionally. Add the vegetable oil and simmer covered for 30 minutes. This is definitely one of those dishes that is made all the better if you drink yourself a few brews or a cocktail while you're doing all that stirring.

LAST WORDS

Well, there you have it pilgrim, the Necronomicon Cookbook, as penned and collected by yours truly, Clifford Bartlett, with assistance (and some conflict) from a long list of slayers and sorcerers, most of 'em now dead and departed.

Next time you're laboring over a hot stove or a smoky grill after a nasty piece of the horror show, tip one back for ole Clifford won't ya?

Me?

I'm goin' fishin'.

Clifford Bartlett

FROM THE AUTHOR

I like to give a shout out to author John Hornor Jacobs, a fellow Arkansas boy, who wrote the book Southern Gods and Neil Gaiman, author of American Gods. A few years back I moved cross-country from Arkansas to Washington state. On the way up, my girlfriend read aloud from Southern Gods.

We found out she was pregnant about two weeks later and decided that the best move for our new little family was to go back south to raise the boy down home. On that leg of the journey she read American Gods. It was a wild month, and hearing those books while we put thousands of miles behind us did something to my brain.

If you have enjoyed this 'cookbook' then I highly suggest you pick up a copy of Southern Gods right away, and later on if you are still hankering for stories about the plight of gods and men check out Neil's novel.

In my mind, as I have been writing this book, it has always had a cinematic quality to it, so if any of readers out there have an interest in working with me to turn this into a film or episodic, please get in touch.

I've been a filmmaker and producer for many years, and would be delighted to discuss the various possibilities of this southern fried world we are sharing.

I also owe much of this book's creation to the wonderful music in which I soaked my spongy soul as I wrote these words. I wanted to take a few moments to present what I've chosen to call the 'Necronomicon Cookbook Official Soundtrack'.

In addition to listing the songs here, I have created a playlist on YouTube, searchable by the same name. I have also done my best to select only videos that have purchase links to the songs themselves, because these are all great artists who are working hard to put food on their own tables and your paid downloads make a difference.

Sean-Michael Argo
seanargo13@gmail.com

NECRONOMICON COOKBOOK OFFICIAL SOUNDTRACK

Jen Titus - Oh Death

Scott H Biram - Blood, Sweat, and Murder

Skip James - Hard Time Killin' Floor Blues

Blind Willie Johnson - Dark was the Night

Slow Train Soul - Mississippi Freestylin

Clutch - I Have the Body of John Wilkes Booth

Creech Holler - Devil's Eyes

The Dead Weathers - Die by the Drop

The Dead Weathers - So far from your Weapon

Black Water Rising - Black Bleeds Through

Highlonesome - Devil at the Door

The Builders and the Butchers - Bringin' Home the Rain

The Builders and the Butchers - Poison Water

The Goddamn Gallows - 7 Devils

The Goddamn Gallows - Ya'll Motherfuckers Need Jesus

Justin Cross - Drink the Water

The Pine Box Boys - Will You Remember Me?

Jayke Orvis - Murder of Crows

The Reverend Payton's Big Damn Band - DT's or the Devil

Curtis Stigers & The Forest Rangers - John the Revelator

Murder by Death - I'm Coming Home

The Unseen Guest - Listen My Son

Monster Magnet - Space Lord

Kid Rock - I Am the Bull God

Mofro - Gal Youngin

Hank III - I'm Drunk Again

Legendary Shack Shakers - Blood on the Blue Grass

FROM THE AUTHOR

Thank you so much for taking this adventure with me, take a quick break and if you liked what you just experienced check out some of my other work.

WASTELAND SURVIVAL GUIDE – Bronco is a gunslinging wastelander of dubious moral character & questionable sanity, and he is here to show you how to survive in the bizzaro apocalyptic future.

BLACK METAL: The Orc Wars – The races of orc, goblin, and troll have been driven to the brink of extinction by the Alliance. A mighty orcish shaman brings the disparate tribes together to form a Horde, and their vengeance will be legendary.

GLADIATORS vs ZOMBIES – A sword & sandal epic in which slave gladiators are pitted against the ravenous undead for the sport of their Roman masters. What champion will rise?

NECROSPACE: A Space Marine Trilogy – A grim adventure alongside the Reapers of Tango Platoon, a group of hired soldiers working in a militarized deep salvage operation in the abandoned scrapyards of a war-torn universe ruled by corporate tyranny.

seanargo.wordpress.com

Printed in Great Britain
by Amazon